I0611629

The Black Spaniard

L.L. Holt

Published by Unsolicited Press.
Copyright© 2016 LL Holt
1st edition trade paperback.
Library of Congress Control Number: 2016941488
ISBN: 978-0-9980872-2-1

Table of Contents

Chapter 1

One of the men in the coach looked about sixty and had a face like a horse. It was a kind face and very dark, though a bit weary. He put his head back and closed his placid, brown eyes, his bushy eyebrows settling into a position of rest. His companion, a highly prosperous-looking bourgeois, was busy making calculations with a small gold pen in a fine-grain leather notebook. An early summer breeze, soft and warm, fluttered the businessman's paper, as well as the loosened ruffles at the older man's neck.

"Don't nod off, sir," the younger man said, tapping his companion on the knee. "We're almost in the electorate. Sorry, sir," he added, with a smile, "no rest, even when coming home."

"Home," sighed the older man. He gazed out the window. "Well, far enough from home, aren't we? Now that France has declared war on Austria, we can expect some changes. We need to be here a few weeks, isn't that correct? I suppose a few more days won't hurt. I hardly know whether I want to go home!" He thought of his dependable, but often nagging wife, the demands of his old students and colleagues who now seemed a part of the distant past. For more than a year he had been absent, working across the Channel in England.

Salomon nodded and tugged absently on his lace cuffs. To judge by the unusually pensive mood of his friend, he knew that the older man was thinking about Mozart.

"I've hardly had time to reflect on the news last year," the elder continued. "It was such a shock, but then, we were so busy with Christmas concerts in London, and I scarcely had a moment to myself." He stifled a small smile as he recalled Mrs. Schroeter, a wealthy widow who had taken a fancy to him. His wife must never know! But memories of Mozart clouded his thoughts. Once again he rested his chin on the inside of his hand, and his eyes ever so briefly misted over.

"Such perfection," he murmured. "We will never see his like again."

"Well, sir, if you'll forgive me, I think he owed much of his success to your own tutelage!"

Haydn snorted. "Hardly! Genius like that comes less than once in a lifetime. No, I had nothing to do with it. It was all the Creator's work! I suppose that is why He took away our boy so early: He must have had designs on him for all eternity."

Salomon said nothing further on the subject and returned to his calculations. "Well, sir, we…I mean, of course, you…did very well by your sojourn in Britain. Take a look at this…"

Haydn waved his hand. "No matter, I'll let you and my accountant go over that. I did enjoy being with the English; they were so appreciative. I think we're taken for granted here in the land of our own language, wouldn't you agree?"

"Perhaps, sir. That certainly was the case with Mozart," averred Salomon. "Look, that signpost. We'll be in Bonn within the hour."

Haydn was underwhelmed. "Count Waldstein insists you audition that young organist we met briefly en route to London. Well, not so young any more…" Salomon recalled.

"Yes, I hear he's around 20 or 21," Haydn said. "Missed his chance at being a prodigy, I'm afraid. Don't know why people keep pushing and persisting, especially when their hour in the sun has gone and will never return again." After a few more minutes of twists and turns, the coach pulled up to the stable compound outside the Electoral palace. "Just as I recall, when we last stopped here," said Haydn, stretching his limbs and wincing at a flash of arthritis in his knees. "Oh, Waldstein, you will owe me one for this!"

The next few days passed quietly, as the Elector, Max Franz, welcomed the esteemed composer to his realm. In turn, the Master gave a private recital for the Elector, including a new piece featuring some of the little flourishes that Haydn had been informed would please and delight the music-loving prince. For, talented musician and inventive composer though he was, Haydn had also mastered the art of patron cultivation and had the purse to prove it.

The handsome Count Waldstein, honored Teutonic Knight who had become a close personal friend of the Elector, kept urging an audition, to be witnessed by members of the Court and their friends. At last a day was selected, and word was sent out to Luis at the von Breuning home announcing an audience with the great Viennese master. As for Haydn, he had seen these Wunderkinder (or in this case, Wunder*mann*) before, and there was sure to be nothing new under the sun. However, he would certainly praise this Court favorite, and, after all, how tedious could his playing be?

The Elector, Count Waldstein, a dozen friends and ladies, some servants, and even members of the orchestra gathered on a mild afternoon in early August. The Chapel Master Lucchesi was seated to the side, and Neefe, Luis's teacher from an earlier time, sat with the band. Neefe had been ill and in recent years had become more involved in local opera and theater than in Court activities, but was well known for his role in bringing glory to the Electorate through his teaching of the young. Neefe had not seen Luis in some time and wondered how he would do. There was buzzing and polite murmuring among those gathered in the hall; a new Stein piano had been brought to the center of the room, and some agreed-upon sheet music spread on the stand. The page turner adjusted his wig, and stood to the side. They waited, and soon the room became very quiet.

"Your Excellency, the composer Franz Joseph Haydn!" announced a footman, and through the main door entered the aging Master, with soft, quick steps and sparkling eyes. He bowed low to the Elector, and then to the others, and took his place at the forefront of the musicians, who buzzed appreciatively. Count Waldstein motioned him over to the side of royalty, however. Haydn paused, since, for all his renown, it was customary for musicians to sit with the servants; but he turned to the musicians, apologized briefly, and sat beside the count.

A low hum of murmuring rose from the musicians, pleased to see one of their own given the royal treatment. But there was also a note of surprise in their whispers, since the Haydn they saw before them was so very different from the great Master they had imagined, at odds with the portrait engravings they had seen all their lives. He was short and small. He was old. But most striking of all, he was very dark.

The murmuring stopped at the sound of a slammed door in the foyer, ringing footsteps from someone wearing hard-heeled boots, and the twin doors to the hall thrown open at once. "Your Excellency," the footman announced, "Mr. Luis van Beethoven."

Beethoven strode into the room. Never had he been in such good health, excellent disposition, so appropriately attired and polished. The von Breunings had seen to it that every detail of his appearance was attended to: his hair had been trimmed closely in the latest fashion, with neat black sideburns; he had refused to don a wig. His maroon jacket, silk trousers and stockings were impeccable, and he pulled off his white gloves with a flashy snap as he curtly bowed to the Elector, and then turned to face Haydn. The two men locked eyes, sized each other up. Haydn smiled and nodded to him.

The young man's dark eyes flashed with good humor as he quickly scanned the room, nodding to Count Waldstein. He was the picture of a young man at the height of his powers and self-confidence.

Luis turned to the piano and sat at the bench as though it were a hereditary throne that no one else deserved. How different from the young man who, five years earlier, stood at the locked gate of the von Breuning house unsure of his future. He touched the keys and released a ripple of scales, a few strong chords. His right thigh tested the knee pedal

"Sir," he said, looking at Haydn, "I will play Mozart's B-flat Sonata, if that is pleasing to you. Then I will play one of my own compositions." There was a murmur of interest among those present.

"Please proceed," said Haydn. The older man had been given copies of the younger man's cantatas, and though a bit raw for his taste, they did show brilliance. He settled in to listen for further signs of talent.

Beethoven paused at the keys for a moment, then launched into a spirited performance, emphasizing the feeling of the piece as well as its inner intelligence. His dynamics were extreme, alternating between whisper-soft passages and the maximum volume the instrument could project. Haydn, who had just premiered his Surprise Symphony in March, with its shocking loud chord after a quiet introduction, nonetheless started on several occasions as Luis pounced on the keys. It was impossible to nod during this spirited interpretation. And yet the heavenly *andante cantabile* of the second movement was spun out seamlessly like a cobweb lingering in the air. *Legato*: the infinite flowing of beautiful sound. The concluding *allegretto grazioso*, so sunny, spritely, and bright, had listeners tapping their toes, nodding to each other agreeably.

At the conclusion, enthusiastic applause greeted the young man, who briefly stood, bowed once, and then returned to the keyboard. "This," he said, "is my sonata in F minor, much altered since its original publication several years ago. I hope you like it."

F minor is a key of dark foreboding, and this sonata contained not only depths and abysses, but also soaring peaks, great gulfs of sound, and rapid passages for strong, nimble fingers. The contrasts were radical, some of the chords jolting to more polite ears. Count Waldstein caught the Elector's eye, and they shared a smile of satisfaction. But Haydn was not smiling.

Under Beethoven's control, the piano, a type known for its quick, spring action and ready response to whatever level of touch it bore, sang a tale of powerful emotions and stormy depths. With the final powerful chords, those present roared their approval and stood quickly with shouts, bravos and eager applause.

Haydn, too, applauded, mildly, and gave the young man a kind, forgiving smile. "Sir," said Beethoven as the applause subsided, "please give me a theme that I may show you what I can improvise."

"I have a theme!" cried the Elector. There was another wave of courtly murmuring, and the Elector rose. "I am very fond of Mr. Haydn's Farewell Symphony, yes, yes, I am, don't apologize, please," said the Elector to Haydn, knowing full well the work was a gentle jab at the composer's aristocratic employer. "That last melody as the musicians leave the stage...very attractive. Do you know it, Beethoven?"

"I'm afraid I do," quipped Beethoven. "Yes," he said, sitting down again, "yes, in fact, that would make a delightful theme!" He rested a finger against his lips, stared at the keys, and was lost in thought. Then, he began to play the sweet, pastoral melody, *soto voce*, and barely audible to those at the end of the hall. The old master's bushy eyebrows rose approvingly, and he almost tapped his foot.

Beethoven, however, had other plans for this melody, and soon marched it through a series of variations, of differing dynamics and coloring, invention, chordal dissonance, and development, flying to incompatible keys, filling the room with miracles of music and dumbfounded listeners. Workers and passers-by outside stopped to look in the window and see the source of such unheard-of sound. And there was young Beethoven, his brown hands flying over the keyboard, caressing the upper register, cajoling the lower, pounding upward and downward chromatic scales in full octaves, his leg crashing against the knee pedal in full force.

With the final signature series of thundering chords, Beethoven threw himself on the keyboard and bounced back like a boxer recoiling from a powerful blow. Then he smiled, showing his beautiful white teeth, as though he had just played the most impish prank on someone and rose to applause that was delayed only because the audience was stunned. But as soon as they recovered, they rose from their seats with a roar and swarmed the young pianist, as a crowd might do at a sporting match. The Elector was beaming, and Count Waldstein went over to Haydn, who remained seated and thoughtful.

"It is new music, I know. It is the future we are hearing tonight, Mr. Haydn." Haydn did not say anything. Mozart was dead. And now this.

"I agree the young man has talent," he said at last, considering all the possibilities. "But new music or not, his talent needs taming. Send him to me in Vienna. I will gladly be his teacher." And so it was that some three months later, Luis would be going once more to Vienna, this time never to return.

Chapter 2

Luis's audition with Haydn warmed not only the breasts of the music lovers present. The charismatic dark stranger shot stormy glances at more than one susceptible young woman in the hall who may or may not have had an affinity for music up until that moment. In fact, a number of fair hearts beat faster during the performance, but not from musical passion. At this stage in his life, and for several years to come, Beethoven was irresistible. Revolution, romance, even talk of free love, were in the air, and Luis was at the right place at the right time. As a young man of heart-stopping presence, in a world of ineffectual aristocrats, Luis was a force to be reckoned with. There was also an appealing reticence about him, due to the reserve about matters of the flesh inculcated in him by his devoted mother. If anything, however, that made him all the more desirable. Yet, who is the man who can follow every deeply cherished principle to the letter in the heat of youth when so pressed upon by opportunity?

Luis was jostled into town in the midst of a half dozen of his closest friends, off to the Widow Koch's outdoor café, there, perhaps, to exchange flirtations with her pretty daughter, Babette, a close friend of Eleanor von Breuning, but so unlike her in personality. They were a klatch of lively, attractive young people, including the Romberg brothers and the artist Kugelgen (without his twin), and though small, Luis stood out. The café was strewn with newspapers and journals, some containing reports of the arrest of the French King, others trumpeting the abolition of slavery, at least on paper, by Denmark-Norway.

A distinguished group of older men were gathering on the far end of the café, including his former teacher, Neefe, who had begun a Reading Society to carry on the work of the banned Illuminati, a group of radical intellectuals he directed for several years. What could be more harmless than middle-aged men reading the latest literature together? Yet in these days of sedition and revolution, any gathering of intellectuals filled regal hearts with alarm. The musicians Ries and Simrock, both former Illuminati, joined Neefe, and soon the men were discussing the audition of their prize former student and "brother." The sky clouded over, and evening fell, sending some inside, others to their homes. The brothers Stephan and Chris walked with Luis back to the von Breuning mansion, Luis's home away from home since his teens. Their sister Eleanor stood behind a curtain, watching from within. She knew without hearing it, that the audition had gone well, and accepted it with satisfaction and with dread. She retired early to her room, with no words of praise for the returning warrior, whose path was so different from her own.

The next months passed quickly. Mrs. von Breuning, the wise and capable widowed mother of Luis's four good friends, used her considerable influence on Luis, prying him away from unsavory potential friendships, guiding his reading and taste for literature, and urging him to complete the lessons he was obligated to give others. She made sure that someone kept an eye on the Beethoven household, so very much poorer than her own, where Luis's younger brothers, Carl and Nicolas, were now in their teens, motherless, with an alcoholic father. For several years, thanks to Luis's intervention, the father had been laid off from his position and his reduced salary had been diverted to the eldest son who managed the family finances from the Breuning home.

Though committed to funding the young man's journey to Vienna to study with Haydn, the Elector expressed no further interest or involvement in Luis's departure. Tensions between France and the German states had reached a breaking point with the fall of Mainz and French seizure of the left bank of the Rhine. Several towns had already canceled their fall musical and theatrical seasons as the threat of invasion became palpable. A small sum was provided to cover the costs of travel, with more to follow once Luis was settled in Vienna.

In late October, Count Waldstein, Mrs. von Breuning, and the young man's closest friends gave him a little farewell party. "You'll be back a new man!" exclaimed Waldstein, sipping champagne in the mansion's great room.

"Hopefully, I won't be back too soon," added Luis, wryly, reflecting on a previous stay in Vienna from which he had to return early to attend to his dying mother.

"No, Papa Haydn will keep you there and put you through your paces," his most enthusiastic patron continued with a wink. "We won't be seeing you for some time…but see you again we will!" Eleanor did not smile, and looked down with a small frown at these words. As much as she wished Luis well in his pursuit of fame and fortune, his absence would create a vacuum in the von Breuning home and a wound in her heart. And yet, with his departure, there was relief, for she did not have to keep him at bay nor disguise her true feelings.

It was a small gathering, and a subdued one. Political uncertainties were on everyone's mind, and there was no saying that Vienna would be a safer place for an up-and-coming composer. As the late afternoon drew on, Eleanor lifted a small parcel off of a credenza and with a shy smile, handed it to Beethoven. "This is something for you to remember us by," she said, lifting her eyes to his. In his usual impetuous manner, the young man ripped open the package, letting the wrapping fall to the floor.

"A remembrance book! How sweet, why thank you, thank you all!" he said with true appreciation, looking around at his friends.

"Now you must read them, read them all!" said Mrs. Breuning, ushering her charge to a divan and pressing him into the cushions. There were 14 entries, only a small fraction of his colleagues, friends and patrons, but they were dear to him. He went page by page briefly, then returned to Eleanor's entry, and read it aloud:

"Friendship, with that which is good, grows like the evening shadow 'til the setting sun of life," Luis read. The group became quiet, and Luis looked up at Eleanor, who was avoiding his gaze. How beautiful she looked in the late October sun, her hair more golden than ever, wound in a braided bun, and her auburn dress, though modest, showing her figure to its best advantage.

"Well," said Luis. "I'll read one other. From you, Count!" The Count looked knowingly at Mrs. Breuning but said nothing.

"Dear Beethoven! You are now going to Vienna in fulfillment of your long-frustrated wishes. The Genius of Mozart is still mourning and weeping over the death of her pupil…With the help of assiduous labor you shall receive: Mozart's spirit from Haydn's hands. Your true friend, Waldstein."

Luis barely read the words, which startled him, for he was not expecting such a testimonial. Certainly, he had self-confidence on his own. But to hear such expressions of confidence from a great man was almost too overwhelming to bear. He coughed to repress a cry, and with great control, put the book down beside him. The room was as silent as emptiness.

"Sir," he said, looking up, his voice cracking. "I vow to live up to your high expectations."

The Count walked over to Luis, dwarfed by the tall figure of the older man, and patted him on the shoulder. "I know you will, my friend. We will be watching you from afar! Remember, you will always have your admirers in Bonn, and we will always believe in you."

The little party came to an end, and with many hugs, handshakes, and final wishes, the visitors left. The von Breuning boys, sensing that Luis would want to speak to Eleanor alone, went to other quarters of the great house. At last, Luis and Eleanor stood alone, breathing in the energy and good wishes, feeling a tangle of bittersweet emotions.

"Luis…"

"Eleanor…"

They laughed to catch themselves speaking at the same time. "Luis," continued Eleanor, looking at her handsome but slightly threatening friend, "Luis, I do wish you all the best. You will learn so much. You have a destiny, a destiny to do great things!" Luis looked at her, perhaps too hungrily. "Luis, do you hear what I am saying? I will miss our conversations, reading books together, oh, Luis," against her better judgment she fell on him in a gentle embrace. "I will miss you."

Luis had been working on mastering self-control, but that embrace—innocent and sororial though its intent—shattered his resolve. "Eleanor," he whispered into her ear with passion, "you must come with me!"

Eleanor tried to pull back, but the powerful arms imprisoned her. "Eleanor," he whispered fervently, "we are meant for each other. Marry me, marry me, Eleanor! I can't live without you!"

Eleanor was alarmed and pushed as hard as she could, with no effect. "Stop it! Luis, stop it right now!" she pleaded.

"We don't have time," Luis said, swinging her around and pinning her to the wall. Her hair became loosened in the struggle, and the braid fell down her back. "I can't wait," he cried, "we don't know what will happen!" He kissed her fiercely as she tried to squirm away.

"Luis, this can't be," she gasped, trying to pry away his strong hands. "God, Luis, stop and listen to me!" He stole one more violent kiss, then realized he had overstepped all propriety and boundaries of decency, and fell back, covering his face with his arm. He lunged at the wall, his back to Eleanor, and sank to his knees. "Eleanor, I'm sorry, I'm sorry." He turned his head and looked over at her form on the divan, her face hidden, her body sobbing but without tears. "I love you so much, Eleanor. We have everything in common. Why can't you--"

"Don't you ever touch me again!" said Eleanor firmly, once she had regained her composure. The fact was, she loved Luis as well, not as a sister, but as a woman loves a man when she is ready to give her heart and life to him. But it was not to be. Forces outside their power, forces that he would never understand, laws he would never obey stood between them.

"I wish you a good journey," she said with trembling voice. "But put me out of your mind and out of your life. Good-bye!" And with that, without looking back, she ran from the room, leaving Luis on his knees, against the wall, his face in his crooked arm, his fist clenched. His heart and body burned, first with desire, then with passion, and finally with embarrassment. Some time passed, and the fever receded. He got up, tucked the farewell album into his vest, and went to his room, which was far from Eleanor's. Luis sat on the edge of his bed late into the night, his head in his hands. What good were ideals and truths if you were rejected, as he imagined, because you are the wrong social class or poor or different looking? It was in a gloomy mood that he slipped off into sleep that night and awoke early the next day, leaving the von Breuning home without further goodbyes, and promptly commencing a journey to the south.

Chapter 3

The ride out was smooth enough, though at a brisk pace in order to reach the city within a week. There was an ever-changing parade of fellow passengers, but Luis was in no mood for conversation. He looked out the window, and sometimes read the literature Neefe had given him before his departure, strange writings from the East and Egypt, which he was careful to hide from the prying eyes of the occasional priest sharing the coach. Among them was a slim volume of a Hindu text translated by Forster. Forster...where had he heard that name before? Luis shook his head to himself. At the age of 21, he had lived so long, it seemed, already had done so much--a lifetime's work! He smiled: and yet, it was just beginning. Thoughts of his old life already were slipping away, and recollections of Eleanor evaporated as the coach drew closer to its destination.

Luis hated to travel and stay in strange places, but most were routine along the way, with one exception. On one afternoon, he was the only passenger on the coach, and the driver stopped for the night in an out-of-the-way inn, very working class, and quite run down. While careless of his appearance and tired from a few days' travel, Luis still cut an imposing figure, and his high black boots, a gift from Count Waldstein, still retained their shine.

After acquainting himself with his room—more like a monk's shabby cell than the sort of lodgings he was now used to—Luis went downstairs for a meal and a pint. The tavern was filled with locals, laborers, and farm hands who had been working hard to prepare the barns and fields for the winter ahead. The light wasn't very good and cast an eerie golden glow over the squalid array of tables and stools. In one corner, Luis noticed a neglected piano, sunk in the shadows. The place had a stale, smoky smell, but he was hungry and eager to just get through the night.

The barmaid took his order. He had nothing to occupy him, no book or paper, and at any rate, one couldn't read in this poor light. So he looked directly into the girl's face, and noticed she was rather pretty, with blonde braids pinned over the top of her head. She in turn looked back, frowned, and took his order.

"Where you from?" she asked, looking at him strangely. "You're not from around here."

"Well, of course not," said Luis, deciding to open up a bit. "I am employed by the court of a prince. And going to another in Vienna." The girl's eyes widened a bit, and she sized up his clothing. Then she smiled, revealing a missing canine tooth. Luis was amused, but maintained eye contact, until he heard a stool shift behind him, and a heavy hand thrash down on his shoulder.

"Darren!" the girl said, annoyed, looking at the hulking shape behind Luis. "Leave off, Darren!"

Darren pulled back on Luis's shoulder and lifted him up with one hand. "Who do you think you are?" The young man was at least six feet tall, with arms like the rear flanks of a large hog, and smelling as sweet. Non-plussed, Luis turned and glared into the man's ugly face.

"Excuse me," he scowled, "have we been introduced?" The tall man was not used to sarcasm.

"Say," he said, tightening his grip on Luis's lapels, "we don't need your kind around here."

"And what kind would that be?" demanded Luis, prying the rough fingers off one shoulder.

"Black devils!" the ugly man said. "Straight from hell, you are!" Luis gave a short laugh, though he was quaking within.

"You are mistaken!" he said. "I am van Beethoven. That would be *van*..."

"He's an arissocrat!" called the bar keep, "lay off 'im, Darren, we'll have the 'thorities here, and I'll loose my license again!"

Darren wasn't so sure. "He's a gentleman, fer sure," said the girl, secretly pleased at the attention, but not wanting anyone to be hurt. "Ain't you, dear?"

Luis unclenched his fists, and drew back a bit, pulling himself up to his full 5 foot 5 height (perhaps 5 foot 6 with the boots), and shook his hair, as though symbolically freeing himself from his assailant. "I am. In fact," he was starting to enjoy the altercation after several days of inactivity, "have you heard of the Chevalier de Saint-Georges?" Blank stares from all around him. "He is a renowned black musician lately in the French court. You might say I am…a German equivalent!"

The tavern owner, impressed, nodded slowly. "It's true about that 'van,' Darren, means royalty," the man continued in a cautioning tone. "So, Mr. Van whatever, don't mind Darren here, he's just stickin' up for his girl, you know how these things is." Luis smiled a superior smile and waved his hand. Had he had a clean handkerchief, he would have waved that as well.

"No trouble," said he, turning to nod pleasantly to the girl, who smiled another toothless grin. "So, let me try your goulash, then, as I see you have a piano, I would be delighted to play you a few tunes of your own choosing!"

The group of a dozen patrons and the main actors in this drama relaxed a bit, and there were hums of approval. So it was that Luis became aware of two other wonderful qualities that he possessed: that of peacemaker among the lower classes, and his own ability to transform into royalty, thanks to the Dutch "van" in his name. The "van" actually meant no more than "of," but in the German states, the equivalent "von" signified someone of royal birth (such as the von Breunings and Count von Waldstein). So what if a small deception were perpetrated; no harm was done. And after all, wasn't Luis *true* royalty, the royalty of genius? It sounded convincing to him, and gave him another tool in his charted course to success.

Predictably, the meal was dreadful, but the bread was filling and the beer enlivening. Before long, Luis was at the dusty piano. He tossed the sheet music onto the floor, and was soon taking requests for "Polly, I wish I'd loved ya better" and "The long night's dark without you, Bess." There were at least six keys missing, and the piano had not been tuned since a wandering furniture hauler had dropped it off some years before.

Still, all had a good time, and soon, Darren was putting a hammy hand of friendship on the shoulder of the man he would have shaken to death an hour earlier. The crowd soon was singing, "I miss you, Mother, how I miss your gentle heart," and a few sobs escaped from the more intoxicated choristers.

At the end of the night's revels, Luis, not overly sober himself, raised a tankard to all present, and said, "Remember, gents and lady, remember tonight, when van Beethoven gave you an evening of music!" "Hurrah!" and similar comments dwindled into the air as the owner closed up shop and Luis made it up to his room, satisfied with a night's work.

Chapter 4

The coach pulled away, leaving Luis and his small assortment of packages and bags on the footpath. He looked up at the grand Lichnowsky Palace, which he had visited briefly five years before. So much had happened in those five years: his mother was dead, his little sister, too; the new friends he had made, the books he had read, the music he had played and composed; the teachers and older associates who had dropped away, like Neefe and his circle. He was a new man. But the palace, indeed, as he turned 360 degrees and took in the view, all Vienna, looked exactly the same. He bundled everything together and walked to the back door. Some day, he thought, the Great will enter through the front, and, in his head, there was no one to tell him to tone down his arrogance.

The room was six flights up, in the attic. Luis sprinted up the stairs, glad to exercise his legs, and tossed his bundles on the bed under a dormer. He paused a moment, looking out the small window over the massive, almost oppressive weight of the cityscape. Born in an attic, lived in an attic: there would be more to his life's story than that. There was not yet a piano in the room, which was large enough to contain one. He looked around to see what would be the best way to bring up such a large instrument. *Why didn't they think of these things*, he scowled.

No matter, for now, the first thing he would do would be to write notes to those behind, including the Elector, to let them know he was safely arrived. He peeled off his jacket and cravat and tossed them on the floor. There was a simple desk with a lantern, a small stove, and a shelf for his books, which he hoped would arrive soon. He put his coach copies—the Egyptian aphorisms, the Indian Gita, a parcel of additional epistles of introduction, all compliments of the banned Bonn Freemasons—on the bookcase, and located the writing paper in the desk. The mid-November sun cast ample light, but no warmth, across the length of the room. Luis blew on his fingers and rubbed his hands together. Well, it wasn't much, but it was a start.

Prince Lichnowsky was out of town when Luis arrived, and just as well, as it gave the young man a few weeks to adjust to his new environment. He soon was taking walks around the city, including strolls along the Danube (which was about an hour away) and the promenade known as the *glacis*, and among the many lovely parks, still pleasant on milder days. He had no trouble finding a practice piano, since the palace was filled with instruments, testifying to his new patron's passionate attachment to the musical arts. And, as his journey had taught him, one could always find an evening's amusement in a local pub, where the hired musician would be only too glad to take a break when a reckless young visitor offered to take over for minutes that would soon spill into hours.

Shortly after the prince and princess returned, Luis was called to meet his new patron in the music room, a spacious parlor with a raised dais on which stood a chestnut colored piano gleaming in the afternoon sun. Luis stared at it a moment, frowning, trying to recall the sense of *déjà vu* surrounding a golden aura around some beautiful chestnut-colored object, but the image quickly passed.

And there was the prince himself, at the keyboard, playing one of Luis's own compositions. "Ah, Beethoven!" he said, lifting his pale hands from the keys, and smiling a warm greeting. "This is really very good!"

Beethoven nodded, "May I?" and sat beside the prince, picking up where his patron had left off and then improvised a half-dozen spectacular variations. All in a day's work!

"Hah, brilliant!" said the prince, beaming, as though in possession of a new expensive toy. "Oh, I so did the right thing. Well, Luis," the prince rose and walked over to a more regal-looking chair with gold damask upholstery, "have you settled in? How is your room? Is your piano in tune?"

Luis fiddled with the keys a bit. "Sir," he said, continuing to play lightly and softly, "I thank you for your hospitality and confidence. You will not be disappointed! But my room is not very satisfactory. And I have no piano whatsoever!"

"No piano!" exclaimed the handsome prince, who was less than 10 years older than his protégée. "Don't tell me they put you in the attic." The prince sighed. "That will never do. We'll take care of that immediately. Ah, Princess!" the aristocrat beamed, as a beautiful woman in her late twenties entered the room. The Princess Christiane was slim, tall, and elegant, with feathers and ribbons woven into a complex hair design, and a burgundy day dress skirting the floor. She was accompanied by her lady's maid.

"My dear," she said warmly to her husband, "please introduce us." There would normally be a slight echo to their voices in a room of this size, but it had been carefully, even scientifically padded and lined to assure a fine acoustical balance, and her voice lingered warmly on the air.

Beethoven was immediately disarmed and overwhelmed by the warmth and generous nature of the princess, and her caring solicitations. Too old to be of interest to him as a lover, too young to be a mother figure, it was more to the latter that his heart tended.

"You will teach my husband, too, I hope," she said with a gentle smile, looking at the prince with genuine affection. The prince took her hand and kissed it softly.

"First," he said, motioning to a servant, "we need to make arrangements for Beethoven's lodging. How does the first floor sound?" Luis was impressed, and nodded his assent. "And I must show you off, I hope you don't mind. Can you prepare a short recital for next week, say, a couple of pieces by Carl Bach, something by Haydn, a couple of your own works, and be prepared to improvise?" He smiled as though "no" was not a possible answer.

"But of course, sir," said Luis with a slight bow.

"Oh, Princess, have someone take Beethoven for a fitting. You'll need some new clothes quickly."

"We'll attend to it," smiled the princess. "I just stopped in to meet you. Samuel will call on you later today about the fitting. Dear," she said, turning to her husband, "No Mozart?" A cloud crossed the prince's face. He had been Mozart's most enthusiastic patron until a dispute over a large sum of money he lent the composer shattered their relationship. Tragically, a few weeks after the prince won a court settlement in his favor in the case, Mozart, overwhelmed with work and cares, succumbed suddenly to death.

A look of guilt swept across his face, and he shook his head slightly. "No, dearest, I am still not ready for that. I cannot feel but I played some horrible role in his demise."

The princess gave him an affectionate hug. "Don't blame yourself, my love," she said. "It was fate. Our lives are not our own, and a person's pathway to success and accomplishment may be cut short at any time by death or some other tragedy. We mourn when greatness is taken from us, when lives are cut short, but life continues, and we must embrace the future while being grateful for the gifts bestowed by the departed."

"Madam," interjected Beethoven, "you are a philosopher. I have studied philosophy at the university in Bonn and have seldom heard such wise and consoling words." He knew he was laying it on a bit, but he was impressed by this beautiful, intelligent woman.

The prince and princess bid Luis a farewell for the moment, and left him to enjoy the piano as long and as often as he liked. After clambering up to his room for writing materials and music paper, Luis returned to the otherwise empty music room, its high white ceiling and walls ornamented with painted vines and roses, and spent several hours practicing, improvising, and composing. Servants came in to light the candles and one chandelier, and asked whether he would like a fire. No, he gestured, for he had fire enough. Such luxury, though hardly noticed.

The recital was a success, with about fifty guests from the Viennese nobility, and a few musicians and merchants in the music industry attending. While enthusiastic about his performances of the younger Bach and Haydn, and appreciative of his original work, it was once again in the improvisation that Luis mesmerized and dazzled his listeners. Afterward, he was embraced, praised, and lionized, accepting the accolades with no embarrassment, as though they were his due. Quite a feat for a foreigner with no pedigree except a few thin letters of reference.

The prince introduced him around, the princess whispered to her lady friends, and Luis was especially interested in some of the attendees he had heard much about before. There was Baron van Swieten, who seldom left his own home: patron of Mozart and Haydn, and champion of J.S. Bach and Handel. And another prince, was the name Lobkowitz? Some count from Russia, someone's beautiful Italian wife, and invitations from all to play at their salons and soirees, offers of halls and assembly rooms, as well as recommendations for instruments (which he cordially ignored).

It was with a cool sense of achievement and success, and perhaps a hint of a smirk, that Luis went back to his new room, a spacious apartment with a modern piano, on the first floor.

What a way to start your twenty-second year (for, in fact, this was the season in which he was born, though he was never sure of the year.) He shuffled through the day's post, and there he found among his letters an envelope with a boldly scrawled address sent by his brother Carl. Luis sat down, took a deep breath, and poured a tumbler of port from the carafe on the window sill. It was probably an urgent request for money. He tore open the envelope, and read something quite different.

"Luis," it began, "you must come home. Father is dead."

Chapter 5

Winter blew quickly over the great city. On the tall green-grey buildings, the fine snow fell, as though shaken from a sifter. Even the shadows were softened by its touch: pale blue, grey, soft green--all tones of the falling white. It was Advent, but detectable only in the bells: a season heard, not seen. Tolling bells like knells for death where no death passed.

Luis had several weeks of freedom before the lessons with Haydn began. That would be quite a commitment, like a full-time position, but with no pay. He wrapped a wool scarf around his neck this late morning and walked out onto the powdered street. He had scarcely been in Vienna a month; already his jacket was shabby. Some people attract physical chaos like a magnet, and so it was with Luis. Saving his good pair for public appearances, he wore old boots he had found in the kitchen; he wore no hat.

There was no question. This time he would stay. Just five years earlier, when studying with Mozart in the great city, he had to leave everything behind to return home to his dying mother, the one person he loved above all others. Now, he walked down Alstergasse, past some high-end apartments, a government building of some sort, a church. Strains of a hymn on the organ drifted into the street and caused him to pause.

The organ. How long had it been? He walked up the steps and inside, striding past the font of holy water, and stood defiantly in the nave. There were not many worshippers at this hour, mostly the elderly, or perhaps they were not human at all, just clumps of shawls, scarves, and caps bunched up over the backs of pews. He stood and listened as the organist, a fair player, filled the space with sound. The music seemed to fill the lungs, the cavity of the head, the body with sound. His mind drifted back to when he was a boy of 11, studying the instrument with Master Neefe, and later in his teens, astonishing the region with his virtuosity. He was surrounded then by friends, the von Breunings, his best friend Wegeler, brothers, cousins, students, his beloved mother. At last, a sexton approached him and touched his arm, rousing him from his reverie.

"Here, my son," he said kindly, placing a coin in his hand, "the Lord is merciful. Get yourself something warm to drink!"

"I'm not a beggar!" snapped Luis, startled back into a sense of the ordinary. He threw down the coin and stalked out. The pew hunchers did not move, the music continued. But there were tears in the young man's eyes, and his cheeks were damp, perhaps only with melted snow. He was an orphan now, without father or mother, and had cast his lot with this great grey city in an unfamiliar land. He was not even sure of his own birth date and was estranged from his friends and brothers, whom he might never see again. Perhaps he had never been part of his family after all, but the son of a prince or king.

When music did not fill his brain, these strange delusions crept in and tormented him. But what the sexton had said about the warm drink struck a responsive chord. He stopped in a café for a cup of strong coffee and to read the newspapers. But even the hot black beverage did little to dispel the oppressive cloud that hung over his heart.

With Christmas and the New Year, however, things changed radically. Luis was performing everywhere in glittering palaces and salons, and in so doing, infuriating the leading pianists of Vienna. This was all to the good, since the dark, young man with the unruly mane of hair and piercing eyes seemed to thrive on opposition and rivalry. His studies with the great Haydn, which commenced in mid-winter—the very thing that drew him to Vienna in the first place—immediately took a distant backseat to an aggressive schedule of recitals throughout the dazzling city, the musical capital of all Europe.

In fact, it was with a sour face and unwilling feet that he dragged himself to the master's studio for excruciatingly boring, tedious, and rudimentary lessons in harmony and counterpoint. How he longed for a close friend, like Wegeler or one of the Breunings, to whom he could pour out his heart. But each smothering episode with the well-intentioned but frequently exasperated Haydn would be followed by a series of brilliant showcases for his genius.

By spring, Luis had developed a formula for bringing audiences—especially their attractive young female members—to their knees. "Luis," said the Prince, beaming over his prize protégée, and offering him a fine cigar after one audience had dispersed, "my dear, Luis, how ever do you do it! Did you see what was happening when you improvised on the Salieri theme tonight?"

Luis smiled, and bit off the cigar tip, tilting his head back for the servant to light the tobacco. "Luis," the Prince continued, leaning forward in one of the apartment's drawing rooms, "they were in tears, weeping! Not just the women, but the men! Weeping at the beauty, the power, the miracle of your playing, your imagination. How do you do it, my boy?"

This was a bit much even for Luis, who turned his head to hide the blush on his dark cheeks. "They are just too emotional, that's all," he said dismissively. "I need audiences that can stand up to great ideas!"

The Prince laughed. "Dear, dear boy, you are turning the world on its ear. Already, you are a different man from the lad who arrived from the country last year." That was true, Luis reflected. Performing in these small recital environments, thick with the smell of beef tallow candles, sweat, and heavy perfumes, with the cream of Viennese aristocracy as his audiences, seemed to have opened a positive version of Pandora's box. The better he played, the more the adulation and applause. The more the adulation and applause, the more inventive and virtuosic grew his performances. His self-confidence, already high, had shot through the roof, and there was no more holding him back than trying to stuff the wild unruly spirits back into Pandora's treasure chest. There was no thought for tomorrow, and no regard for yesterday.

For Luis had slammed the door shut on his past. Though pining for a close friend with whom he could share his triumphs, he was divorced from the world of the Bonn court, from his now-dead parents, from the Elector who now seemed so petty and insignificant. His teachers—he could hardly remember their names. Even Neefe, though he cherished the Illuminati and Masonic texts his former master had entrusted to him. The great ideas he culled from Neefe and the library of the Breunings, those remained and had taken root so that he would always love Plutarch and Homer, and follow the modern poets, Schiller and Goethe. But over all else, he was drunk with the radiance of his own rising star, a creature whose genius, forceful personality, country accent, and strange appearance gave Viennese society something to talk about.

Such talk, however, included the mumblings, curses, and gossip of erstwhile darlings of the recital stage. "I hear you've been playing a bit roughly at the baron's," Haydn said in passing one afternoon.

"Roughly, what do you mean?" said Luis.

"Too much emotion, not enough attention to form!" the master said sternly, though with his trademark smile.

"Emotion! That is what music is about!" stormed Luis.

"Calm yourself, young man," corrected Haydn, pushing him lightly with his finger tips to the piano bench. "You'll never amount to anything if you let your feelings get the best of you!"

Many were the times that Luis wanted to flee those lessons in counterpoint, the art of pitting melody against melody without incurring discord. In life, as well as in music, Haydn had mastered this art. In conversation and negotiations, he was a genius of polite expression, never upsetting an antagonist's position, and resolving all arguments with good feelings for both parties involved. While learning to master musical counterpoint, Luis, however, made no effort to incorporate the lessons of tact and delicacy of sensibility in his daily life. For him, all conflict was a call for battle, not a minuet of sweet sounds and moves creeping point by point to a harmonious resolution.

Soon, however, he would have no more reason to long for conflict as the most arrogant pianists of Vienna challenged him to war.

Chapter 6

The first of these occurred early in his Viennese years in the form of one Abbé Gelinek. Before Luis came on the scene, the Abbé was the reigning lord of the piano in the musical city of a quarter of a million souls. About a dozen years older than Luis, with high cheekbones, tussled golden hair, and a kindly though somewhat condescending expression, the ordained priest was beloved throughout the city for his performances and improvisations. And as competitions between pianists were the vogue at that time, it was inevitable that the Abbé would challenge Luis to a musical duel.

The Abbé, whose patron was Count Kinsky, had a loyal following, and met with a few friends to invite them to the event to be held in the Lichnowsky music room.

"Who is the other pianist?" one of his supporters, a white-wigged conservative, asked.

"Oh, I don't know, some nobody from up north," the priest replied affably.

"Are you afraid of losing?" asked another, mostly to tease the unsurpassed master.

The Abbé laughed, then his face assumed a look of dark foreboding. "I am going to *pulverize* him!" he declared. The Gelinekians roared their approval and left their friend to practice his drills.

The night of the contest arrived. It was hot, as Vienna often is in the summer, and it was the first time Luis had been exposed to such heat. He took one look at the Abbé and smirked. The Abbé took one look at Luis and politely stifled a chuckle. Ah, thought the Abbé, a scruffy boy, probably a mulatto: mere child's play. Another feather in my cap!

The Prince had arranged for two pianos to be positioned back to back, so each instrument could entirely absorb the personality of the performing artist, and to provide a home base for each pianist as the other played. There were easily 100 guests crammed into the hall, including members of the press, and a few aristocrats in search of new talent to patronize.

The two artists came up to the dais, bowed to each other, then to the audience, which was in high spirits and already given to applause. The bulk of the cheers, of course, weighed in with the popular Abbé, in intimidating ecclesiastical dress, who bowed more deeply in a demonstration of superior humility. It was agreed that the event would consist of three "rounds," beginning with variations on a theme provided by the opponent, then each playing a work of his own composition, then an extravaganza of improvisation.

Beethoven won the coin toss, sat at the bench, flipped out his tails, such as they were, and winked at two pretty girls in the front row. With one hand, he carefully played an operatic tune, and could it be possible that he exaggerated a few pauses in deference to his opponent's aging ears and memory?

Gelinek smiled affably, played back the melody note for note, then launched into a series of non-descript variations that sounded more like a child's exercises in theory. Beethoven smiled to himself, leaned back just a bit, and a couple of times raised an ironical eyebrow. *Such harmony, such delicacy of tone*, the priest's sympathizers purred among themselves.

At the conclusion of the performance, the Gelinekians shouted "Bravo!", while nodding to each other knowingly and, occasionally, elbows jabbed the ribs of the person standing nearby. The warmth of the candlelight, the oppressive heat of a summer evening in the city, and the growing excitement among overdressed concert-goers made for an increasingly toasty experience. When the applause subsided, it was Gelinek's turn to propose a theme, and he played a delightful tune by Mozart (who, it was widely known, had once spoken favorably of the priestly pianist). He, too, exaggerated certain phrasings for the benefit of this newcomer.

Luis rattled off the tune perfectly, even further exaggerating certain phrases, and cast a furtive glance at the audience. What was it about audiences that brought out the best in him?

Luis loosened his collar (an unheard of act of undress in public) and dove right into a series of breathtaking variations, the first so daring and unexpected, the audience gasped. He developed the theme to its maximum potential, right up and into the second variation without a pause. In this variation, he exploited the piano's range and sonorities to the fullest, with crashing chords and flying arpeggios that no one could believe a human being could execute. Ladies began fanning themselves furiously, and the men were struck dumb.

A third variation, soft, delicate, mournful, made it seem as though the instrument contained an immortal soul, aching for heaven. Then another rush of octaves and ninths, a peaceful interlude, and a concluding thunder of pianistic gymnastics. Luis concluded the set with a series of crashing chords, followed by a soft recollection of the heavenly strains heard earlier, and then a single "da-DAH!"

There was silence. Utter, complete, total silence. Then a man in the rear shouted, "Bravo!" and soon the entire assembly was on its feet, shouting, and applauding. Luis smiled to himself, nodded to the Prince who was trying not to burst out laughing, and looked around the piano lid to catch the astonished expression on the face of his opponent.

"Well," said the Prince, acting as a kind of impromptu emcee, "on to Round Two! Father Gelinek, please enchant us with your own composition of choice!"

The Abbé was not looking quite as robust as he had when he first entered the room. In fact, his right hand was shaking. He wiped his forehead with a handkerchief, and looked almost shyly at the audience. He could not see Luis, who was sitting uncomfortably on his bench, fascinated by little circles of soot on the ceiling. In profile, the two men gave onlookers a study in contrast: the young man on the left, dark, disheveled and perhaps a bit impish; the older man on the right, fair, delicate, and ecclesiastically aloof.

Most of the good Abbé's compositions were variations, one of the simplest musical forms. He had selected one of his "Potpourri" series, with a nice conventional opening melody followed by variations featuring plenty of 32nd notes (to showcase his speed) and little flourishes so popular in the court (to highlight his sensitivity). The performance was predictable, although his nerves began to take their toll in the final runs. He concluded quietly, and attempted a weak smile to his well-wishers, who responded at first hesitantly and eventually more warmly in good fellowship.

"Are you done, Abbé?" called Luis across the instruments. A titter of amusement swept through the audience. More fans appeared, and some women were sharing them with their mates or dates.

"I am," said the Abbé with a shaky voice.

"Then I will play my new Sonata in g minor, still a work in progress," announced the younger man. He turned to the keyboard, eyes sparkling, and soon filled the hall with haunting sounds of longing, mystery, reclamation, and dreams of an ideal world. The audience was transported, and more than a few sobs were heard during the masterful rendition of the haunting slow movement.

Not only was Luis's playing transcendental: the music itself was like nothing that had ever been heard before in Vienna. At the conclusion, Luis took a theme from each movement, and wove a number of virtuosic variations on each. Again, the audience went mad, and the Prince for a moment feared that all propriety would be lost with the storming of the stage, so he and a number of his colleagues rose to protect the performer from the onslaught of good wishes.

"Well," beamed the Prince, again. "Another impressive performance! Do we have enough stamina left for Round Three?"

At this, the Abbé, as discreetly as possible, withdrew from the stage, taking a round-about route to the rear of the music hall.

"It does look as though Mr. van Beethoven is going to indulge us in yet another extemporaneous performance!" The Prince actually drew back at the volume and intensity of cheers. This time Beethoven asked the audience for themes, and as they were called out, he selected the ones that best showcased his superhuman abilities, weaving legatos, fugues, and complex variations that glistened in the air like the musical equivalent of spun gold.

At the conclusion, the hundred or so guests had been joined by late-comers, servants, neighbors, and even the occasional passer-by in an almost riot of excitement and emotion. Luis was nearly lifted off his feet, and it was only the quick thinking and nimble actions of some footmen and a stable hand who had wandered in that whisked Luis possibly out of harm's way, into the safety of the palace, where he was able at last to laugh long and loud, at nothing in particular.

The next day Gelinek, shaking his head, told a close associate, "I will never forget yesterday! The devil is in that young person. I have never heard such playing! He improvises on a theme I gave him as I have never heard even Mozart improvise."

That was all that was needed. The word was out.

Chapter 7

"Well," said the Prince one fine day in the New Year, "it looks as though you may be getting a secret invitation!" Luis was at the piano in the rear salon, making corrections to a manuscript. "Oh?" he said, not looking up, with his usual disregard to royalty or his employers. Probably another pianistic "duel." They were sort of fun, but a little went a long way.

"I know what you're thinking," said the Prince, who seemed to have little better to do than to dote on his increasingly notorious charge. "You're thinking that I want you to exert yourself like an athlete bringing down all the grand pianists of Vienna, while you want to just stay here and touch up old manuscripts! Am I right?"

This was annoying, and he wasn't going to get any work done, so Luis pushed the pad and pencil to the side and turned to face the Prince. "What is it?" he asked directly.

"Hmm, hmm," hummed the Prince. "Should I tell? Well, it is secret, but word is out among my former lodge brothers that the True Harmony lodge may be having a little reunion. You know about the True Harmony, I trust."

Indeed he did. Neefe had mentioned it in his final letter to him, urging him to find and associate with its former members, although for the most part, they had been mere Masons, not Illuminati. "You'll never find wiser and more helpful men," Neefe had written, "and you may be surprised to find some great thinkers and artists who are women in their midst."

As instructed, Luis had destroyed the letter, since Joseph II had banned secret societies of all stripes in 1785. While there was some tolerance to Freemasonry, since certain lodges were composed of none other than lords and other aristocrats, membership in the Illuminati, with its radical revolutionary cast, was punishable by death. If only Professor Adam Weishaupt of Ingolstadt could have foreseen what the future held when he created the Bavarian Illuminati in 1776!

"I have heard of True Harmony," answered Luis noncommittally.

"Did you know I was a Freemason when it was still legal?" the Prince asked. Luis was surprised.

"Really, sir!"

"Shhh!" said the Prince with a wink, "don't tell anyone. Yes, we had an entire lodge in Vienna composed of Princes and such. A fine group it was, too, but for talent, my boy, there was nothing like True Harmony! Haydn, Mozart, the geologists de Born, Sonnerfels, and Forster..."

"Forster, sir? Would that be George Forster?"

"One and the same! I see you know your science as well as philosophy. You must have had some fine teachers at the University of Bonn!" *More like the University of von Breuning*, thought Luis.

"Yes, and glorious writers and poets, some of Austria's finest: Blumauer, Alxinger, well, you may not yet have heard of them all, coming as you do from the Land of Goethe!" The Prince smiled. "Well, what does all this mean? It means," he said lowering his voice conspiratorially, "that the True Harmony is staging a reunion! As a pupil of Haydn and, if memory serves me correctly, of Neefe, you should be able to wrangle an invitation. In fact," he produced a little note on princely parchment, and rotated it among his long white fingers, "I have here a secret pass to ensure your participation! But really, see if you can go with old Haydn, it will ease your entry into this gathering of giants!" he winked again, and placed the note between two leaves of music paper.

After the Prince left, Luis looked at the note, and a thousand thoughts flooded his mind. What a great opportunity to meet the intellectual leaders of the Austrian Enlightenment! And Forster…yes, the name triggered an immediate recollection. There was a family connection there he was not likely to forget. Luis was also quite certain this was the same Forster who translated the works of Egyptian and Indian mystics, which nourished his soul on many a cold winter's night. He had, in fact, copied a phrase from that book and kept it under glass in his room, to remind him that the Divine was not the province of one ancient nation in the Middle East, but belonged to and was celebrated by people of spirit in all parts of the world.

All of the names the Prince had rattled off were linked not only with art, ideas, and science, but also with revolution. How odd, yet reassuring, that a Prince in these times would support the notion of liberty! Especially considering the news earlier in the year that the King of France had been beheaded by the people he had served. Perhaps the presence of great musicians like Haydn among these leaders affirmed that music could play a role in the liberation of humankind and in the perfectibility of man. For the first time, Luis could hardly wait to get to his lesson with Haydn the next day.

Haydn was waiting patiently as Luis arrived, threw off his overcoat and dashed into the practice room. "You certainly seem eager today," mused Haydn, "what has inspired this enthusiasm for augmentation and diminution?"

"Sir, will you be attending the True Harmony reunion? The Prince asked me to represent him, and thought it would be kind to welcome you as well," said Luis, molding the facts to his own advantage.

"While I have you in an enthusiastic mood, let's proceed with the lesson, then we'll talk later." This irritated Luis, but he complied, since it would only work to his advantage to arrive with Austria's premier musician, whether or not he actually deserved to be so regarded. And if any raids and arrests should follow, he would no doubt be safer in the company of Papa Haydn than in the proximity of any radical revolutionaries.

There was someone in Vienna whom Luis had not met, but needed to. This patron of the arts—a composer of note in his own right—had been an active Freemason in the heyday of True Harmony. Luis soon learned it was at this notable's home that the reunion would be held. And so, at last, he would meet Baron van Swieten.

Unlike other titled aristocrats whom Luis had met, the Baron was a working man. His father had been physician to the Empress, and, after a Jesuit education, the son became a diplomat with many successes in Western Europe. Following a brilliant career in civil service, he was appointed Imperial Librarian, a position of great status and influence, and one he maintained for his entire life. Among his many accomplishments, he invented the world's first card catalog system for libraries.

As he traveled through the German provinces, Poland, and other nations and principalities, the Baron indulged his passion for music, studying with some of the finest teachers, and cultivating an enthusiasm for the works of Bach and Handel. Soon he was commissioning works from Mozart and Haydn, who enjoyed the support of this well-to-do and singularly knowledgeable patron.

Unbeknownst to Luis, the Baron had been present during his duel with Gelinek. The Librarian was looking for new musical talent to nourish and cultivate, and that is exactly what he found.

Although secret societies had been banned, there was a fairly liberal attitude among Viennese officials regarding the Freemasons. After all, many of them had been active members, and benefited from the social and intellectual stimulation it provided. So no one felt particularly on edge about arriving at the Baron's home for what may have appeared to outsiders to be a grand party (though somewhat lacking in female participants). Former Masons, and those who considered themselves Brothers for life, or members of "Reading Societies," arrived openly at the Baron's door and were admitted without subterfuge. Singly and in pairs, the gentlemen (and, yes, a couple of women) ascended the steps leading to the bachelor's well-appointed home, and soon a carriage discharged old Haydn and his protégée into the night.

The Baron's home was not as lavish or extensive as a Prince's palace, but held its own as a bastion of civilization and cultured values. There were beautiful paintings on the walls (including a Vermeer), tasteful furniture, and endless shelves of books and manuscripts of musical scores.

Luis sized up the room, then the other guests, trying to imagine who were the scientists, who the philosophers, and so forth, since small groups immediately broke out. As to the Baron's identity in this mass of intellects, there was no doubt: he was the tall, commanding figure in the center of the room greeting guests and making sure everything was going smoothly. He was around Haydn's age, a bit more portly, but nimble, with large expressive eyes and quick, bird-like movements. There were rumors he seldom slept, and it was not hard to imagine him up all night regaling guests, playing music, or devising schemes to change the course of music history.

As for attire, it had been decided that forgoing Masonic aprons, chains, and symbols would be a good idea. Although most of the Masons present did not wear wigs, the Baron did, and a powdered one at that; his overall dress was about 20 years behind the times, but sumptuous and of the highest quality. And the heels of his boots were just a bit too high for fashion or comfort.

As a trio played something by Cimarosa, the sharp-eyed Baron spotted Haydn, and his glance and breaking smile immediately turned to the small slender man beside him, the young man with the restless black eyes and Spanish appearance.

"Aha!" cried the Baron, striding in their direction, leaving a pair of geologists to fend for themselves. "The destroyer of Gelinek! The successor to Mozart!" Haydn did not particularly like to hear this, but smiled politely and bowed to his patron. "Yes, yes, I was there, you know, at the 'duel,' yes, and quite an unforgettable impression you made, young man!" he effused, putting both hands on Luis's shoulders and steering him around the room. Haydn resignedly joined a group of poets, who welcomed him warmly.

"Yes, yes, the man of the hour!" trumpeted the Baron, so all could hear over the trio and general buzz of conversation, "the next great musician to grace our great musical capital!" Luis nodded regally, though he hoped silently that he would not have to play just yet, or maybe not at all, since he was hungry to meet the Brotherhood, network, and to have something to eat. "So, young man," he continued, pulling Luis over to the side, "I need to see you in private, to hear you play. I can tell you've studied Bach, am I not correct?"

Luis nodded, "Yes, Your Excellency, I was brought up on the Well Tempered Clavier."

"Excellent, excellent!" exclaimed van Swieten. "And what about Handel?"

Luis shrugged. "A bit here and there, mostly religious pieces I was required to play."

"No no no no!" exclaimed the Baron, in mock horror, while he attempted to disguise a chuckle.. "We'll see what we can do about that," he said jollily. "What do you do on Wednesday evenings?" Luis could think of no steady occupation. "Then you must come visit me, every Wednesday, is that a deal?"

"I suppose so," said Luis, who actually was warming to this Dutch aristocrat, "except for a trip with Haydn to Eisenstadt this summer, and unless the Prince has other plans."

"Prince, Prince," pooh-poohed the Baron. "Say, we are nobility on our own, aren't we, *van* Beethoven?" he whispered, then laughed. Luis smiled awkwardly, and rather hoped that subject wouldn't come up. "Well," said the Baron, "I won't tell if *you* don't! We Dutchmen must stick together. Now, young man, suppose you get yourself something to eat and drink and then I personally will introduce you to some of the guests. What you do with that knowledge is totally up to you!"

The affair was extremely informal for that era, and Luis was relieved not to have to sit at yet another long table and wonder which fork to use on the mussels, and try not to knock over the red wine (it was always the red that was spilled). For a few minutes, he enjoyed hanging back from the crowd, and wandering about with a plate of dumplings, nodding to one of the musicians whom he had seen several times in town. The Baron was continuing to greet a stream of visitors, though Luis never left the corner of his eye, not for a moment. At one point, however, Luis wandered into the folds of a burgundy velvet curtain and was shocked to discover he had stumbled upon a seated lady.

Chapter 8

"Oh, ma'am, I am so sorry," said Luis, blushing, and straightening out the drapery folds. *Please, God, do not let me pull them down on her,* he silently begged.

"Hello," said the woman, "that's all right. Thank you for stopping by and talking to me. It's been rather lonely here for the past 20 minutes!"

There was a chair beside her, so Luis sat down, and put his plate on the floor. "You're not from around here, are you?" she asked. Luis was still getting settled.

"No, no, I'm from the north, from Bonn. Say, don't tell me you are a Mason!"

The woman laughed. "Hardly," she said in a low voice, "though close to it. There are only a handful of composers in this group, and I think the Baron invited me to swell the number of musical representatives. 'Too many miners (meaning geologists)!' he's often said about True Harmony." The woman smiled a small, stiff smile, as though it was not something that came easily to her.

As usual, Luis was preoccupied with his own agenda, but began to relax into the moment, and looked more closely at the woman. She was obviously a gentlewoman of high status to judge by her elegant dress and elaborate hair style; and he had learned to look at people's feet to learn much about their lifestyle and social rank. But when his eyes drew up to her face, he paused. She had a porcelain-pale complexion, and deep-set blue eyes, but they seemed unfocused, did not blink, and there were dark circles, unusual for someone who appeared to be in her thirties.

Then it hit him: she was blind.

"I can tell you are staring at me now," she said, as though this was often the case when she met people. "It's all right, I'm quite used to it, but do continue your conversation. Unless it's about the manufacture of odoriferous sulphur compounds or some other scientific nonsense!" She ventured another stiff smile.

"Oh, I'm sorry, I was just looking for Haydn. Do you know Haydn?"

She uttered another vague laugh. "Yes, but not as well as Mozart," she said, "God rest his soul."

Beethoven actually was getting a little tired of hearing about Mozart, but wanted to know more about this woman. "I met Mozart," he said. "How do you know him?"

"Why," she said, "he dedicated his B-flat major piano concerto to me!"

Then the lantern flame went off in Luis's head. "Don't tell me!" he fairly gasped, "you're not…Maria Paradis?"

Maria was enjoying the reaction. "Yes, my dear man, I am one and the same. I have committed just over sixty piano concertos to memory and performed throughout Europe. I have commissioned works by Salieri, Mozart, and others, though now I devote most of my time to composition: cantatas, operas. Are you a musician and composer by any chance?"

Luis could hardly believe his luck. Here he was having a private conversation with one of the most celebrated composers and pianists in Austria, and a woman to boot. And blind! And he thought *he* was different! "Composer…yes! In fact, I've written two cantatas…"

"And where were they performed?"

Luis sighed. "They were my most ambitious work," he said, "but never performed. The musicians, the singers, they could not handle the difficulties, and so it was that the day of the Emperor's coronation came, and other works were substituted."

Maria nodded. "A familiar enough scenario," she said. "Don't take it too hard. But I heard the Baron allude to your duel with Gelinek. I do not duel," she said, with a note of irony in her voice, shifting one pale hand on top of the other, "but can appreciate what a remarkable achievement that must have been! I hope you will play later."

"I hope *not*!" said Luis, and they both laughed. "I hope to write opera," Luis said.

"Well," his new friend confided, "you'll want to seek out Salieri as your master. Haydn is fine with sonatas, symphonies, and religious works, but you need an Italian soul to compose opera in Vienna!"

Luis filed this information in the back of his brain. Hidden by the folds of the curtain, the two musicians talked and talked, and time flew by. Luis talked about his love of the newly developed, larger pianoforte, and his aspirations to compose more complex works. Maria told him about her affection for her doctor and how she was forced to end treatments.

"My dear young man," she said, reaching out and feeling for his hand, which he willingly gave her. Her sensitive fingers felt the palm, like a fortune teller, and she noted the wide flat fingertips and deep calluses. "I hope misfortune never befalls you, and you may have a long and happy life. But if affliction does come your way, do not fall into melancholy or despair. I wasted many days of a precious life feeling sorry for myself…"

"As well you might!" said Luis, placing his other hand on top of hers, and also noting the strength of the fingers.

"No, this is important," she said, with some urgency. "Whether it is a love affair gone wrong or some personal tragedy, do not let it destroy you. Let your intellect and your spiritual depth guide you. Do you read the classics?"

"I do," he said, "as well as classics from the East."

"That's not surprising, given your interest in Freemasonry," she said. "Be a musician, be a composer," she continued, "but above all, be a philosopher and an open-minded, open-hearted child of God, however you chose to define him. That will get you through the hard times, even if they are as overwhelming as the hard times I have faced, being blind and a woman." She smiled without humor.

"Young man, what is your name?" she asked.

"Luis van Beethoven," he said.

"Van Beethoven. I will remember that name. Mr. van Beethoven, I think your friends are missing you. Why don't you join them? I will not stay much longer, my friend should be here shortly. Sir, it has been a pleasure talking to you. Remember what I said. Salieri, for opera. Great thoughts, for survival. All my best to you."

Though he was not accustomed to doing so, Luis lifted her hand to his lips. "Thank you, my lady, and best wishes for a fascinating life!"

Luis rose and took one final look at the poised woman seated before him, and walked back into the room. A number of gentlemen nodded and introduced themselves, attempting conversation, though none was the match of Maria Paradis. Luis in turn shook hands, stated his name and occupation, and then caught Haydn's eye across the room. He was about to cross the floor when the Baron spotted him.

"There you are, Beethoven, where have you been all evening? Let me introduce you to Dr. Reinhold…"

"Sir," said Luis, "is George Forster here? I must speak to him."

"Forster, Forster…oh yes, the Captain Cook adventurer," recollected the Baron. "No, I believe he is in Paris, sorry to disappoint you. Paris! What a god-forsaken place to be! What man in his right mind would willingly go there and risk the guillotine."

Luis was crest-fallen, and said, "Sir, if you don't mind, I'll just circulate, you need to attend to your guests." At that moment, Blumauer, the editor and satirist, cornered the host, and Luis slipped away without detection. Former Masons had spread out throughout the downstairs, and it was easy to find other hiding places where he could withdraw, think things through and decide who, if anyone, he wanted to approach.

As he was thinking this, he felt a firm hand fall on his shoulder, and a voice—a deep melodious voice with a foreign cadence—fell upon his ears.

"Excuse me," said the man who appeared to be an Ethiopian noble in splendid African dress, "do I know you?"

Chapter 9

"No, sir," said Luis, "I am Beethoven, the pianist."

"I am most pleased to meet you," said the African, making an unusual bow that involved touching his fingers to his lips and forehead. "A musician! I am acquainted with your Haydn, and have known Mozart." Luis frowned. The "M" word once again! "I am a former member of the True Harmony," the white-robed man continued, "and my name is Angelo Soliman."

Angelo Soliman! Even in Bonn, he was a living legend. Neefe had mentioned him on several occasions, and Ries had made a comment regarding him that eluded Luis at the time. Luis did not know what to say, and for once, he was fascinated to meet someone who would offer him no particular advantage, either as a patron or a musical insider. Meeting and talking to people from different backgrounds enlarged his own experience, feelings, and how he thought about the world. His imagination quickened.

"Sir," said Luis, "it is an honor to make your acquaintance. Were you not the Grand Master of the Lodge?"

"Very good," said the gentleman, with a subtle smile. "The Viennese are a fickle lot, and few recall my service in that. As an outsider, perhaps, you, too, have noticed how people here, how do you say it, flow with the tide?"

"I'm afraid not," said Luis, "My days are taken up with lessons, teaching, and wooing patrons, leaving me little time to observe human nature."

Soliman laughed to himself. "Human nature. Yes, you will find it in abundance here!" he said. "I sometimes wonder whether the dissolution of the Lodge had less to do with politics and more to do with the peculiarities of my leadership."

"What peculiarities?" asked Luis.

"Surely, my appearance, what is considered my 'exotic' background, but more than that," Soliman mused. "The Lodge had become a place of superficial society, gossip, that sort of thing, not worthy of the Masonic tradition. I proposed to reform the Lodge and steered it in the direction of scholarship, connoisseurship, critical analysis of world events; in a word, scholarly discourse. Scholarly discourse in Vienna! Imagine that!" The Moor shook his head. He studied Luis for a moment and narrowed his eyes. "Surely," he said, "you must have encountered some experiences in your life relating to your skin color and unusual features!"

Luis felt a jolt go through his body. No one had ever been so direct with him on this subject. At the same time, a thousand recollections of derision, restriction, and abuse raced through his mind, and he sank into one of the dozens of elegant chairs placed around the perimeter of the room.

Soliman looked down at the young man, noticed his pock-marked face, the shaving cuts, the unkempt hair, the hastily tied cravat, and short hands already, at this young age, covered with a mat of dark hair. He noticed the broad forehead and nose, the forward slope of his jaw.

"My dear young man," he said, sitting down beside him, "I fear I have upset you. Please forgive me."

"No, no," said Luis, whose imploded posture gave quite the opposite message, "It is true, of course it is true." He looked closely now at the man before him, and said, "My entire life has been touched by my otherness. From my birth, to my profession, to my ill luck with women, to simple matters of business and commerce. I find myself followed in shops, and suspiciously watched, as though I were about to make off with a pocket watch or even a pair of game hens!"

Soliman could not stifle a soft laugh, and he patted Luis on the shoulder. "But I was thinking not of negatives, but of the benefits," the African exclaimed. "You have done well for yourself in life, already at this young age," the African said. "Surely you are not from a rich or royal family…"

Luis was about to protest that there were rumors he was an illegitimate child of royalty and that the "van" in his name had aristocratic connotations, but he thought better of it.

"Black men in white society—or even men who are simply darker than the norm—may face obstacles, but I like to think they have advantages, including a shared history of wisdom, perhaps an inner sense of organization and ability to synthesize, and a natural predilection for achievement," Soliman said in his beautiful, rolling voice. "Just look at yourself. I hear you are a success, another Mo…a singular talent on the concert stage."

He paused and reflected, then said, "We foreigners need to be better, don't we. We have to surpass our own personal best, time and again. Well, for some that is simple enough. For someone who is aware of their roots in the great Continent and its community of souls, it is not difficult to be great in this…" he waved his hand gracefully to indicate the hall, "…superficial world of minuets and bon bons!" Luis frowned, but it was a frown of understanding and appreciation, a new way of looking at his world.

"I hear you defeated the priest!" said Soliman, in a lighter tone. "Word travels fast where Gossip is King. You will be fine, I am sure, as long as you keep your edge. Don't let anything happen to distract you and pray for good health! In my own case, a good marriage has been my saving grace, and as a high-level servant and intellectual advisor, I am able to maintain my place in society with minimal interference." He arranged the folds of his spotless robe, trimmed in a thin ring of ermine. Soliman wore an equally brilliant turban, and had a gold ring in his right ear and several on his dark, graceful hands.

"Sir," ventured Luis, "are you from Ethiopia? I know little about Africa, except a Biblical reference to that country, and to Egypt, thanks to my teachers." This time it was the African's turn to frown and consider.

"I am from Nigeria," he said, "and I began life, as a child, as a slave."

Luis swallowed hard, and the words were out before he could stop them: "I know what you mean! I was a slave, too." A wave of coldness fell between the two men.

"You were not a slave," said Soliman in icy measured words. "You have no idea. No matter how shackled and abused, you were not ripped from your mother's arms, locked in irons, and herded onto a slave ship with thousands of others whose only crime was being born in a land easily accessible to those driven by greed and cruelty."

"I'm sorry," said Luis, as memories of sketches of the slave trade he had seen in the von Breuning's library came vividly to mind. "I know, the words just slipped out…"

"Those were your true thoughts," said Soliman, "but while we serve the Truth, we must be certain we know what is true before we utter it."

He took a breath, smiling slightly. "Come now, no harm done. You may read of my story, it is widely published, so I'll say no more about my history. You may look at me, Luis, and ask, how is this man different from me, other than surface details of dress and deportment? I will tell you. You may be dark, but you were raised in a white culture with white attitudes. I was raised in the Great Continent, steeped in its culture and lore, nourished by its forests and fields, and a body of philosophy, literature, and music that came deep from within the culture and was shared orally and in the details of life, every day, with each member of the community. We did not go to Church on Sunday: each moment was a Mass of Celebration, and Nature was our high priest. The rhythms of life pulsed in our music, and it was never ending. We had a spirit of brotherhood that your culture only now is beginning to experience.

"You have something of the appearance of blackness, but do you have its soul? Only you will know. I can say this: if you study our scriptures and literature, our symbols and wisdom, you will be a better man, a better musician for it. This is what drew me to Freemasonry. In its mysteries, I found a hint of not only my own origins, but also the origins of all mankind. And remember: though the Brotherhood may be banned at present, it will live forever. It lives now."

Luis could say nothing. He remembered Neefe's instruction, the book of wise sayings from Egypt and the East, the symbols, the Illuminati rituals derived from Masonic tradition. He recalled his own insinuation into the Illuminati when he was a young adolescent, read the rites by Neefe, the Bonn Illuminati director, and by Simrock, the hornist and publisher, also a leader in the group. The candlelight, the sacred knives, the words of invocation in a forgotten tongue...

Layered over his understanding of Western thought, culled from conversations and lessons at the von Breunings, and his brief term in philosophy at the University of Bonn, Luis began to understand. What Soliman said, seemed so right. His own otherness had not been so much the cause of his problems as a pathway to their resolution. Embracing the culture would take him closer to the Goal; and perhaps that was the "G" in the Masonic logo.

"Tell me," said Soliman. "When did the world begin? What were you taught?"

Luis thought for a moment, trying to remember if he learned that from the Jesuits or from Neefe's Masonic calendar. He was never good at history…or math.

"Was it around 5,000 B.C.?" he asked.

The corners of Soliman's lips turned up ever so slightly. "So your teachers would have you believe," he said. "Yet at that time, the civilizations of the Great Continent were thousands of years old. And they have never been matched for greatness in every area of human endeavor. Read the words of those people, study their images if you want to achieve greatness in any field."

Luis drank in Soliman's words, but a cloud hung over his heart as he realized how different they were from all the teachings he had known. "Sir," he said, "there are those who insist that blackness is a sign of inferiority. How do you deal with that?" He was thinking of some of the racist secret society members, such as Meiners, who had branched off into their own narrow world of hatred and ignorance.

Soliman's face became profoundly serious. "I know, there are two camps at war in your Enlightened society: those who believe in the equality of all people, perhaps even to the overthrow of kings; and those who wish to categorize and prioritize people by race to their own advantage. Did you ever hear of a Chinese or African who regarded the white race as superior? Of course not. In fact the Chinese word for Westerners may be translated as 'barbarian.'

"Luis, European society is playing a dangerous game. In recent years, scientists have studied the different human types. I am no authority on this, but try to remain as current as I can. It is sometimes difficult without the active support of the Brotherhood. We have had Brothers such as Meiners and Spittler, who claim white superiority and provide fake science to back up their claims. Their supporters are thankfully in a small minority. Then there is the majority view, including the recent shift of the philosopher Kant to this camp: the viewpoint that all people are equal, and that differences of appearance can be attributed to climate and geography. The racist argument was founded on the false idea that the skulls of Africans and the skulls of Europeans were of different calibrations. But Blumenbach actually measured skulls in a controlled and systematic way, and discovered there were as many variations in the one race as in the other.

"Well, we have gotten ourselves in a rather heavy discussion," the older man said. "I must be moving on, and I see that your companion is growing restless across the room." Luis looked up and saw Haydn looking as though he wanted to escape from the clutches of two long-winded natural scientists.

"Thank you, sir, I've learned a lot, and I'll be sure to follow through with your reading suggestions," said Luis, rising. "It's been wonderful meeting you, and do know that though I am a newcomer to this city, you may regard me as a friend and confidante if you so choose."

Soliman was amused at the young man's self-confidence and obliviousness to the older man's rank and station. He nodded slightly.

"Keep that spirit, young man," he said, unsure whether he really had made an impression or simply provided an hour's entertainment. "You will need it in this world filled with adventure and intrigue."

They shook hands, and Luis joined Haydn, whose eyes widened with delight, perhaps for the first time, upon seeing his young charge.

"Sir, isn't it rather time we left? I have work to do early tomorrow, and I am certain you must be tired." Luis took his teacher's arm and somewhat forcefully extracted him from the scientific conversation. Haydn looked curiously at Luis. Why this sudden concern, he wondered, the scamp must have something up his sleeve.

"Thank you, Luis. May I suggest we make an inconspicuous escape? You will find out soon enough what it is like to try to say farewell to the Baron!" The pair eluded their host's attention, though Luis would return to van Swieten's at a later date. But as for Soliman, their paths would never cross again, except obliquely under unimaginable circumstances.

Chapter 10

Haydn announced that he was taking Luis along to Eisenstadt for the summer, to a small house reserved for him near Prince Esterhazy's family castle. The current prince, Nicholas II, who had been Haydn's patron for several years, was not expected to be in residence at the castle as it was rumored he kept a brothel in the city with dozens of mistresses to keep him occupied.

The carriage ride was half a day's journey south, through a pass in the Leitha Mountains. The small town lay flat and peaceful on a plain filled with farms and a patchwork of crops.

The two men enjoyed a relatively cool summer and many opportunities for Luis to wander in the woods not far away. He was finishing up his set of three piano trios, which would become his milestone Opus 1, while Haydn was busy ingratiating himself to the court and working on his so-called London symphonies. The plain grey house where they stayed was within easy walking distance of the Baroque castle, which had more of a palace's appearance, being rather boxy with four stories and two rectangular towers. A magnificent church from the same era, with terraced roofs cascading from three sides, occupied the center of town. There were many opportunities to play and to hear music at a leisurely pace. And yet, there were no friends, no society. Luis had, of course, his books, his music, but how he longed for the sympathetic companionship of the large number of friends he had left in Bonn! First and foremost, Wegeler, who was now a medical doctor and professor at the University; the Kugelen twins, the Rombergs, Tony Reicha, the von Breuning brothers. Eleanor. Eleanor above all others. He fell to musing about her, his heart full of the romantic intensity that was just beginning to make its presence known in the Germanic lands, and began composing a set of piano variations. His thoughts grew warmer as the weather cooled, and his time in Eisenstadt was nearing its end.

The too-quiet summer eventually turned to fall, and soon the two musicians' sojourn came to an end. Returning to the city with bundles of music manuscripts under his arm, Luis was greeted with much fuss and to-do by the Prince and Princess, their guests, and a growing number of hounds and lapdogs. A large box of correspondence awaited him when he returned to his apartment, and before he was properly settled, he began writing a letter of contrition to Eleanor.

"My highly esteemed Eleanor, my dearest friend," he wrote, "A year of my stay in this capital has nearly elapsed before you receive a letter from me, and yet the most vivid remembrance of you is ever present with me. I have often conversed in thought with you and your dear family, though not always in the happy mood I could have wished, for that fatal misunderstanding still hovered before me, and my conduct at that time is now hateful in my sight. But so it was, and how much would I give to have the power wholly to obliterate from my life a mode of acting so degrading to myself, and so contrary to the usual tenor of my character!" He paused, dipped his quill into fresh ink, and continued.

"Many circumstances, indeed, contributed to estrange us, and I suspect that those tale-bearers who repeated alternately to you and to me our mutual expressions were the chief obstacles to any good understanding between us. Each believed that what was said proceeded from deliberate conviction, whereas it arose only from anger, fanned by others; so we were both mistaken. Your good and noble disposition, my dear friend, is sufficient security that you have long since forgiven me. We are told that the best proof of sincere contrition is to acknowledge our faults; and this is what I wish to do. Let us now draw a veil over the whole affair, learning one lesson from it: that when friends are at variance, it is always better to employ no mediator, but to communicate directly with each other."

Luis carefully tucked a copy of his variations on a theme from the *Marriage of Figaro* with additional conciliatory words, and wrote the address he knew so well on the envelope. Was Bonn really that far from Vienna? And yet it might as well have been on the other side of the moon.

It might well have been. Luis was now pulled into a maelstrom of circumstances that only his own inner resources, and wellspring of musical ideas, could survive.

"Luis, come here, I have news for you," Haydn stood at the door outside Luis's room, where the young pianist was writing thoughtfully in pencil on a loose sheet of paper. It was now winter, and the young composer was a sorry sight in his thread-bare grey sweater and two pairs of trousers, layered to save on heat. Luis did not look up, to Haydn's annoyance. "Luis!" The younger man slammed down his pencil, having had just enough of his elder's insistence on immediate obedience.

Haydn lifted a letter and shook it at Luis, but with a sad cast to his eyes. "I was not able to persuade your Elector to provide additional support for your studies," he said, handing the missive to the younger man. Luis grabbed it in disbelief and read it twice through before crumbling the paper and throwing it onto the floor.

Then the impact hit him hard. "Damn!" he exclaimed, hitting the wall with his fist. "What am I supposed to do? How can I live?"

Haydn's features melted into an expression of compassion. He walked over to the young man and put a comforting hand on his shoulder. "Don't worry, my boy," he said. "We have our differences, but you will not be abandoned. Pay me back later, when you are able. And you *will* be able to, I have no doubt."

Luis refused to look at his benefactor's face, his own skin flushed with embarrassment. "It's not your doing," Haydn reassured him. "The French are taking over Bonn. The Elector and his court have fled. I'm afraid nothing that you remember from your childhood remains."

Luis nodded, still not facing his teacher, then walked quickly from the room. What kind of life was it for a man of conscience? To be dependent on petty royalty and then one's own teacher. He had nothing but his own wits to protect him, and who could say what cruel trick of fate would intervene with illness or accident? A musician, no matter how accomplished, was at the mercy of fate and wealthy patrons. Society regarded musicians and composers as servants required to enter aristocratic homes through the back door along with tradesmen. If something happened to his Prince, he'd be playing the piano in a brothel or pub, if he were lucky enough to get the job.

Turning his back abruptly on his teacher, Luis pushed on the heavy door and lurched down the steps onto the cobblestone street. He walked quickly into town, warmed by the crush of other pedestrians, and found refuge in a coffee house. Soon, Haydn would be back in England, charming well-heeled businessmen and doting aristocracy with his conventional tunes. Luis, on the other hand, was ready to explode, and wanted all the world to hear it.

But Luis was at his best in adversity, a condition he was familiar with since birth. As winter wore on, he relied on his genius for performance and composition, his charismatic personality, new connections, and pure aggression, sweeping through the early years in Vienna with one concert triumph after another. In his absence, Haydn had transferred instructional duties to the pedagogue Albrechtsberger, who, though strict, inculcated in the young composer a profound understanding of counterpoint, the art of pitting note against note, melody simultaneously against melody. Luis was at last mastering the tools of his compositional trade. In the language of the Masons, he had passed his apprenticeship and was entering the third degree.

Soon even his homesickness was relieved. His brother Carl arrived in the spring, and Luis was happy to help his sibling become settled in the unfamiliar land. By the fall, friends from Bonn—Wegeler, Lorenz von Breuning, the Rombergs who stopped by en route to their new jobs in Hamburg, the Willmanns with their pretty daughter Magdalena—began arriving, though none would stay permanently. Although she did not leave home, even Eleanor became part of his life again, renewing their correspondence and sending him little hand-made gifts. Luis thrived on these friendships, and warmly embraced his beloved colleagues from the past.

So between new and recent patrons, some teaching of the daughters of the nobility, and even the first revenues from composition, Luis was able to make a go of it. He continued to give recitals in local salons, though few were the pianists who challenged him to a technical show-down. His powerful hands were filled with improvisational marvels, his brain swam with musical ideas for sonatas, trios, songs, concertos, symphonies. He was seen regularly at local taverns enjoying meals with his friends, laughing, sharing stories, engaging in flirtations, or earnestly discussing republican politics. He was in sync with the revolutionary spirit of the age, the growing swell of Romanticism which, like a great cultural tornado, swept up the rational ideals of the Enlightenment and enrobed them in the warmest expressions of human passion and deep feeling, though not without a path of destruction in its wake.

Encouragedby his still faithful patrons, Luis engaged on a tour of Prague, Dresden, Leipzig, Berlin, spanning another winter and a spring season, lining the young composer's pockets, for the first time, with gold. From the Golden Unicorn, an inn where his prince and Mozart had stayed some years before, Luis wrote to his brother Nicolas, "My art is winning me friends and renown. What more do I want? And this time I shall make a lot of money." His reputation as a performer but also a composer to be reckoned with, spread beyond Vienna throughout the German-speaking world, but there were unresolved issues in the past that would rise to haunt him in the future.

One of these was the death two years earlier of George Forster.

A naturalist and explorer, Forster had been exiled because of his radical political convictions, and died of illness in 1794 in a sordid flat in the Rue des Moulins in Paris. Despite his contributions to natural science and literature, he died alone of a stroke, in squalor and disgrace, but not without leaving some eloquent artifacts behind. When his room was being cleaned out, a minor official was called in to take a look at certain written materials. They did not seem to impact the revolution in any way, but had perhaps some value to those opposing slavery, still recognized by the government in transition. These documents were notebooks entrusted to him by Luis's cousin Rovantini more than a dozen years earlier. Living with the Beethovens at the time, Rovantini, a cousin on the mother's side, died while trying to learn more about a shocking racial experiment taking place not 200 miles from the Beethoven home. Rovantini's passion for justice was his undoing, but the notebooks in which he and a colleague recorded their observations in written testimony and sketches had been sent to Forster for his protection and eventual action.

Because of the disruption caused by political chaos in France and the German states, the Reign of Terror, and the war in Europe, the notebooks, while recognized as of interest, had no immediate relevance to those who discovered and processed them. They therefore began a journey to return to their source, which would take nearly three years to complete. The notebooks came perilously close to annihilation in Kassel (the site of the experiment, in which enslaved Africans were studied to establish theories of white supremacy). The books were smuggled into the University, lay fallow for nearly two years, were revived and sent to Bonn, and throughout a bizarre series of activities and coincidences, wound up one morning in the daily post at the Viennese apartment of one Luis van Beethoven.

By this time, Luis was 25, the musical celebrity without equal in the Austrian capital, and a force to be reckoned with. His German and Czech tour had been an artistic and financial success. Throughout Vienna, his music was discussed, debated, and analyzed, often soundly trounced in the press, but mostly celebrated for its daring and innovation. Stretching the very definition of music as it was then known, his work signaled a radical break with the past and seemed to point the way to an unstable but thrilling future. As his friends returned home, Wegeler to a post at the University of Bonn, Christopher to his beloved family, Luis filled the void with more music, score after phenomenal score flying from the pens of copyists and printing presses. Luis continued to master his craft, maintaining an ambivalent friendship with the patient Haydn on his return, but no longer a pupil of the senior master.

There were thousands of Viennese, and those throughout Europe, clamoring for new material, and he could barely keep up with the demand. Despite a few setbacks in his health—some stomach distress, a buzzing in his ears, those damn headaches—he persisted with energy and passion, though he was becoming short-tempered and even less tolerant of stupidity and human error, feeding off the adulation of his public and believing perhaps he was invincible. The old lessons about Divine Providence, the teachings of religion and even Masonic quasi-spirituality, were laid to rest. Men were masters of their own destinies, and God, if he did exist, was the servant of human intelligence and action.

Shortly after returning from a short concert trip to Bratislava, Luis received a package through the post. He was expecting to see a set of proofs or perhaps a manuscript from another young composer looking for guidance when he tore off the paper and string from the package that arrived that late autumn. Instead, he saw something utterly unexpected. A shock, a distant memory touched his heart as he lifted the two battered notebooks and the wrappings fell to his feet. At first, he was flooded by memories of his cousin Rovantini, then Neefe and his strong conviction that the notebooks had great meaning.

Luis looked at the writing, some smeared and difficult to read on the brown pages, crisp, wrinkled, and water-stained. The books tended to fall apart at the spine, and he quickly placed them on a table, ruffling them further with his calloused fingertips. Perhaps the memories they brought back of his own adolescence were more compelling even than the tale they told. Luis had suffered as a child, not only from his father's strict teaching methods, but also by bullying for his appearance. He was small, untidy, and dark complected, so much so that he was sometimes derided by his blond classmates. Even his dearest friends teased him by calling him, "the Spaniard" or "our black friend." For Luis, the issue had evaporated with his success, but here, for the first since Soliman's comments at the True Harmony reunion, was a reminder that not all people who suffered discrimination were as fortunate as he.

He glanced at the horrid images in the notebooks, images of people in chains and in pain. What would he do? Did he have a responsibility? Where was this going? It was so long ago, the experiment, supported by a landgrave who had aided the Hessians in the American war, had surely come to a halt. There would be nothing left but a ghost town where once the moans and cries of oppressed people had rung. He thought deeply about his next steps for some time. Then he knew what he would have to do.

He would entrust the notebooks to Angelo Soliman.

Chapter 11

Luis had not seen Soliman since the Masonic reunion several years before. Still highly valued by the Viennese aristocracy, Soliman had had no visible public role of late, and rumor had it that he was in poor health, though Luis had seen him at several of his own concerts and recitals, his white robe and turban brilliantly visible in the otherwise dark, candlelit halls. Luis decided to send the notebooks directly to Soliman. He would know what to do.

The climate for equality had never been better. Hadn't France, rocked as it was by conflict and bloodshed, banned slavery in all its possessions some years before? Weren't there new abolition movements in Britain? Haydn had told him as much. And what about the leading writers of the time? Luis had not kept up with the issue as much as he would have liked, but it was as clear as that this new general, Napoleon, could become the Washington of Europe. Equality for all was a matter of fact, and would soon be a matter of policy. No thanks to the Church. No thanks to Divine intervention, if such a thing existed.

In the next few days, Luis repackaged the materials, with a note, and did some detective work to find Soliman's address. Then, with one final moment holding the manuscripts, released them to the carrier, and went on with his day's work.

It was a dark autumn day, cool for this time of year, when Soliman's servant brought the package to the ailing Moor. He frowned as he noted the return address, and his servant snipped the roughly knotted twine from the paper. Soliman coughed, a hacking cough, and returned to the settee where he had been confined of late. The servant quietly removed the outside paper, and lifted the two notebooks and note from the wrappings.

"What are they?" his master asked.

"I do not know, sir," said the servant, thumbing through the pages slowly and deliberately, "but there is something disturbing here."

He brought the books to Soliman, put a clean cloth on his master's lap, then placed the books on it. He bowed and left, removing the wrappings and putting them in the fire. Soliman began to read, and as he read, he became agitated. The writing awakened long dead memories in this man, who may have been a Prince or Lord in his native land. His coughing increased, but when the servant reappeared, he shouted at him to leave, and uncharacteristically, threw a nearby book of poetry at the unfortunate man.

"Get out!" shouted Soliman, who picked up the cloth containing the books and, bent over in pain, carried them to the credenza beside the fireplace. He was cold and shivering, but the fire in the grate was no match for the fire now raging in his brain.

"What is this? What is this?" he repeated to himself. "This cannot be. This cannot be." Scenes he recognized, recalled, had hidden in his memory for a lifetime, rose up like daggers in his heart. Soliman gripped the sides of the books with all the force of his body, as though by pressure he could squeeze the reality away, the memory of torture, the memory of his mother dragged off in chains. The fire reflected in the diamond brooch he wore on his headpiece, his eyes blazed in the agitated light. The experience of years past, the dread and guilt over his serene life away from what should have been his responsibility, convulsed his body, and taking both volumes in his hands, with a great roar, he heaved them into the fireplace, releasing a cloud of smoke and cinders, and he fell with a crash, taking the contents of the credenza—all porcelain and silver like that from the Habsburg Palace—with him and on him as he collapsed onto the floor. The servant ran in again, and called for help, but it was too late for help, for Soliman was in a fit of some sort, and it would be a matter of hours before a medical doctor arrived and pronounced it a stroke. And before nightfall, Soliman was dead.

When Luis heard the news a day later, he was stunned. Then he thought of the notebooks and a cold wave of fear swept over him.

"Did they find anything…anything unusual, any odd packages?" he asked van Swieten during a Wednesday evening visit. The Librarian, now an enthusiastic patron of the young composer, shook his head sadly.

"There was nothing. He was sitting on a couch, his servant heard a shout, rushed back, and found him thus," van Swieten said. "You will have to play me something funereal this evening, my son, something with poignant variations to bring tears to my eyes but solace to my heart."

But other thoughts were on Luis's mind. The servant, he reflected, day-dreaming through van Swieten's panegyric. The servant might have a clue as to the current whereabouts of the notebooks. It would be smart to pay a visit to the dead man's dwelling before it was cleaned out. So Luis played for van Swieten and managed to lull him to sleep, a rare event indeed, allowing Luis to escape earlier than usual. The next morning, he went to Soliman's rooms, but there was a terrible crush of visitors and official-looking vehicles. Not sure what was going on, Luis wove his way through the enclave and managed to find someone who appeared to be in charge.

"I hear that Lord Soliman has passed," he said to the director, who was supervising the removal of furniture and property. The man looked dismissively at Luis.

"Out of my way," he said, "we've got business here!"

Luis persisted, "I want to speak to his servant! I was an acquaintance of the deceased."

The man smirked. "Back door!" he said pointing with his shoulder, since his arms were full of linens and a folded tapestry. Then he turned his back on him. Luis was annoyed, but determined to find the servant, and squeezed through another group of merchants, as well as mere onlookers, as tragedy has always been a spectator sport. With some effort, at last he made it to the servants' entrance, and walked in unimpeded. The door led to a kind of mud room which opened into a storage area, followed by a rough kitchen. There at a table sat two young men, one hardly more than a child, one as dark as Luis, the other fair. Luis sat down with a sigh, as they looked at him in surprise.

"I need to talk to the servant who found the Master," said Luis firmly. The two looked at each other.

"Why?" asked the fair boy, "He's done nothing wrong."

"I just need to know if the Master received a package before his attack, it's very important. My…my own…friend. The, uh, friend of my employer, yes, that is it, he sent it and urgently demanded I learn its whereabouts," Luis said, finding it not so easy to improvise with words.

The dark servant nodded. "That was me," he said. "Yes, a package arrived, just that day. Master didn't open it, he threw it in the fire," the young man said.

"What!" Luis rose to his feet, unable to believe his ears. "What! In the fire….show me that fire, show me the room!" Then realizing he was making matters worse by shouting, said, "Please excuse me, I am still upset by your Lord's death."

"I'll show him, Tommy," said the fair boy, and motioned to Luis. The pair, with Tommy walking behind, wound their way through the apartment that was in a terrible state of commotion and disarray.

"Here's the room," said the fair boy at last, "that," pointing, "is the fireplace." Luis rushed to the grate and knelt in the dust before it, unmindful of his clothing. He grabbed an iron and poked at the residue. There was nothing.

"Wait," said Tommy, "over here!" Luis looked in a far corner of the grill, and there was a tiny piece of paper with a fragment of an address on it. He couldn't be sure, but perhaps it was a remnant of that package.

"And here," said Luis, starting to see what minutes before his eyes failed to detect. Another scrap to the left, having fluttered outside the fire, with an image of a person's foot. It looked to Luis as though the package had been opened: the wrapping cast to one part of the fire, the notebooks to another. But there was no other trace. He rose to his feet and roughly brushed off his pants.

"This will have to do. I am convinced you are correct, though perhaps he did open the package first and what he saw may have caused him to toss the contents here. You have my thanks."

With that, Luis pocketed the two scraps, and departed, with a worried look on his face. He stopped at one point, and watched from the side as the beautiful apartment of Angelo Soliman, strung with the finery of Egypt, cherished artifacts from Nigeria, and elegant pieces of Meissen and Limoges, was reduced to a dust-filled shell. Who knew who were the true dealers and estate merchants, who were tricksters making off with what they could? Was this how life ended for people with high social status, who may not have family in the immediate area? And what of his remains, where was his body now? No doubt in some funeral director's parlor awaiting the rites of a Church he did not believe in and interment in a grave not of his own choosing.

In this latter regard, Luis was quite mistaken. In fact, a significant contingent of the home invaders he passed represented the interests of Emperor Franz II for the Imperial Court Cabinet of Natural History. Although Soliman's daughter had returned to the city immediately upon hearing the news, her pleas with the authorities were ignored. The interests of Imperial Science must be served.

In the view of the Emperor and his Director of Collections, Soliman was not a scholar, tutor, intellectual, and cultural leader of his time. He was a curiosity. Moreover, he was a representative of a Type. The ashes in Soliman's fireplace contained a story that now was being played out again in the world of men.

For in the weeks to come, it became known that the African's corpse had been delivered to the Museum rather than the morgue, and fell under the knife of a taxidermist rather than of an undertaker. And in one of the most sickening acts of desecration in the history of so-called civilized humanity, the body of Angelo Soliman was gutted and stuffed, and put into a loin-cloth with beads, a headdress, and other "savage" appurtenances. Then this specimen was displayed in the Natural History collection with the similarly desecrated bodies of two other Africans, along with a lion and a tiger, in a kind of diorama depicting life forms in darkest Africa. And it would be there still had there not been a fire in the mid 19th century which destroyed it and the entire contents of the hall.

In this way, Luis, who was sickened when he heard of the mutilation of his acquaintance's remains, saw that behind the seemingly friendly and welcoming smiles of the Viennese majority, in at least some cases, echoes of racial hatred and notions of white supremacy resounded. He looked in the mirror and wondered what shocking surprises awaited him in a city where such horror could be condoned. As long as he maintained his edge, he was ahead of the game. But one false step or unanticipated affliction…he shuddered and left his room abruptly, going for a long, vigorous walk to flush the dreadful prospects from his mind.

As his pace accelerated, it was almost as though he left the new Luis behind him; gone, at least for now, was the cocky show-off, the brash, hot-tempered virtuoso. With each faster pace, he seemed to step back in time, craving someone to confide in: Neefe, his mother, Eleanor, a friend (for all his friends, including Wegeler, had returned to the north). But sometimes, a fast walk can serve as a substitute for speaking with any friend, and so it was he slept soundly that night. During the weeks ahead, as winter approached and Luis was soon a year older, he retreated to the wisdom literature he once had loved so deeply, and the Prince noted a new seriousness in his manner.

Chapter 12

"Well," said the Prince, "let's not be too gloomy. Winter is bleak enough!" to which Luis frowned and said nothing. His reading now was the classics, particularly Plutarch and Homer, with the writing of Egypt and the East a close companion. It was at this time that he copied another anonymous Egyptian text from George Forster's translation, framed it like the previously saved quotation, under glass, and set it at his writing table:

"I am that which is. I am all that is, that was, and will be. No mortal man has lifted my veil."

What did it mean? To Luis, the answer was in its ambiguity. The deaths of Soliman and Forster had thrown him into a reflective mood, one in which he was open to classical wisdom, the possibility of a Divine Presence in the lives of men, and the tenderness of love.

As the days grew shorter, word came from Paris that General Bonaparte had returned in triumph, making republican hearts beat a little faster and causing monarchs to shift a bit uneasily in their satin slippers. Luis continued to perform and compose-- premiering his Mozart variations in December, but a somber mood of "all work and no play" seemed to haunt the young pianist-composer. With no friends, other than his cheerful patron, to distract him, he became more aware of the digestive problems that had long plagued him and the annoying popping, buzzing noises in his ears. Had he simply inherited the hypochondria of his old teacher, Neefe?

Apparently not. Neefe, in the prime of life at age 49, died suddenly in Dessau that January. The news hit Luis hard, especially since he had made light of his teacher's influence in recent years. And another blow: in April, his beloved friend Lorenz von Breuning, having successfully completed his medical studies, went to his grave at age 21. Not even spring, the season Luis cherished above all others, could heal his broken heart.

"Luis," said the Prince, one day in late spring, at a loss as to how to cheer up his investment, "look here," waving a newspaper, "this is a nice little concert you might enjoy. A Mozart quartet, some Cherubini. Several of my string players are going, why don't you join them, it will take your mind off whatever dark musings have occupied you of late." The Prince smiled, eager to inspire a good mood in his favorite. "I hear the new teacher of the Mozart children plays first violin with them and is quite good."

What did he have to lose? Luis agreed and joined the others, but they were all delayed at dinner at The Swan (Luis preferred to eat in town rather than follow the rigid ceremonies attendant on the Lichnowsky dinner hour, which also was at the ungodly time of 4 o'clock). While the musicians ate in the dimly lit tavern, a tall young man attempted to interrupt their conversation.

"Excuse me, sir," he said, addressing Beethoven, "I would love to introduce myself."

"Go away," snapped Ignaz, "can't you see we're eating?"

The young man persisted, "I tried to talk to you last week, do you remember?" Luis ignored him, and tore a fist of bread from a loaf without looking up.

"Away, away!" added Moshe, "some privacy please!" The young man bowed and backed off.

"The penalty you must pay for fame!" said Ignaz, digging into a plate of spaetzel and pork.

Luis grunted, as his mind was on other matters. "Yes," he said at last, wiping his lips, "I do want to hear that quartet. We're not too late, are we? Are you with me?"

"Not I," said Ignaz, "too much good food, and I want to enjoy what I pay for!" Luis laughed, slapped Moshe and the cellist Harper on their backs, and left the tavern while it was still light. He double-checked the address, and found himself before long at the Hofrath house, where a local family hosted small musical groups.

Mrs. Hofrath recognized him immediately as she opened the door. "Mr. Beethoven! What a pleasure, we are just setting up, do come in!" the bubbly young woman said.

Luis forced a smile and entered the parlor, middle class but with above-average good taste, where she guided him to a seat just behind the first violinist's chair. After 10 minutes or so, during which several people approached Luis to compliment him on a performance or one of his recent works, the quartet settled in, and began playing Mozart's E-flat quartet. A number of candles were positioned around the room, though not sufficient for the musicians to see their scores clearly.

The lead violinist, a young man with excellent posture and limpid blue eyes, was clearly having difficulties seeing the notes, and had to adjust his music stand several times. But a helpful hand reached past him and turned the page, not just for the first few pages, but throughout all four movements of the work. It was as though the wind had blown into the room at exactly the right moment, page after page, so there was no break in the flow of the music and the synchronicity of the four players, who soon were playing as one.

In fact, the violinist became so used to the page turner, he did not at first think to thank the mystery person who helped him perform so beautifully. After the applause died down, though, he blushed to think of his oversight and turned around. There was Beethoven, with a knowing half-smile on his face.

"Maestro!" the violinist exclaimed and took his hand and kissed it. "Maestro, it is you!"

Now, Beethoven knew he had seen this young man, roughly his same age, perhaps a bit younger, somewhere before. There was something majestic, to him unforgettable, about his posture and height, the way he carried himself, the nobility of his gentle features, his clear eyes so blue one did not notice the deep pock marks of his complexion.

"The restaurant!" said the violinist and smiled openly. "Yes, I was the pest!"

"You're not a local, are you?" asked Luis, a question that had been put to him so many times. What was that accent?

"Ah, my accent!" said the violinist, "it always gives me away. Sir," he bowed low, "I am Karl Amenda, your servant, lately of Latvia and recently graduated from the University at Jena!"

"Ha!" assented Luis, nodding, "a fine school. I myself studied philosophy at Bonn. And your field?"

"Do not laugh," said the self-effacing violinist. "Lutheran theology is my subject, and my family proposes I enter the ministry."

Luis nodded noncommittally. "So, you play very well," said Luis, "I have studied the violin all my life, and my playing still sounds like alley cats in heat." They both laughed at the image. "So, you have two more selections to play tonight. I look forward to hearing you…and your colleagues," he added, gesturing to the others who were hanging on his every word. "We can talk later."

The quartet played beautifully in the second half of the concert, and Luis felt a strange prickling at the back of his neck. He felt something shifting, as though the city, perhaps the earth itself, was moving beneath his feet, almost imperceptibly. It was a familiar, if rare, feeling that occurred when a mood and worldview was changing, signaling a kind of sea change in his body chemistry.

Mrs. Hofrath had rearranged the candles, and a page turner was no longer required, so Luis could sit and watch and focus. At the conclusion, the four men shook hands, said what they would have done differently, and complimented each other as members of the small audience crowded around them.

Luis stood off to the side by himself, observing, especially watching the tall young man with the violin tucked gracefully under his arm. How noble his brow! How sincerely concerned he seemed with each person, no matter how humble, who spoke to him. There is dignity, which shoots up through a man or woman, imbuing their every gesture with sincerity, integrity, and grace. This dignity was Karl's. So different than the stuffy aristocrats, coy hangers-on, and rough-and-tumble musicians Luis dealt with each day! Gradually the gathering dispersed, and as Mrs. Hofrath put the room back in order with the help of a servant, Luis waved Karl over to a set of chairs to continue their conversation. It was now quite dark in the room except for a couple of candles flickering from the movements of the mistress.

Karl was so pleased, so happy at last to meet the man who was being hailed as the next great composer of Vienna, and already a pianist without rival. Indeed, he had nothing further to say. Instead, he looked at him a long time. Luis almost blended into the blackness, with his dark skin, hair, and black coat. A pastor by inclination as well as training, Karl noticed the rough skin of Luis's face, bathed in candlelight, in a sense like his own, scarred from a serious encounter with smallpox. In fact, the texture gave interest to Luis's intelligent, unusual face. But mostly Karl looked into Luis's black eyes, with a golden candle flickering and glowing in each, as though the light shot out from within his head.

"And so," said Luis, "You want to meet me, and now you have nothing to say!"

Karl laughed. "I suppose I just want to play more music!" the violinist said.

"That sounds like a wonderful idea!" exclaimed Luis, a flood of energy sweeping over him. "Let's do that, together. I live not far from here, do you have any other engagements?"

"Why no," the other said. "My friend Mylich is at the rooms we share, but he will be long asleep."

"Good! Then let's go off to my place, I have stacks of music by all the greats, including some new works, not just mine, either." The two men grabbed their overcoats, said good night to Mrs. Hofrath, and left the house.

The evening passed in conversation as well as music. Luis wanted to know why a pastor from Latvia was playing the violin in Vienna (he was taking time off to pursue what he most loved before committing to his career), and Karl asked why Luis was not devoting more time to composition (he was simply in greater demand as a pianist; and it certainly was better for paying the bills).

"Will your landlord complain at our playing at this hour?" asked Karl, hanging his coat and jacket behind the door. He couldn't help but notice the mess throughout the apartment, strewn with scores, instruments, open books lying face down, a half-finished lunch.

"The beauty of Vienna!" sighed Luis, illuminating the room. "It is one of the few places in the world where one can make music every night and hear only words of praise the next day."

He poured Karl and himself each a glass of red Hungarian wine and rooted through a box of scores until he found something suitable. The two men played, and drank, and talked the night away. Never had Luis felt so uninhibited in the company of another. Never had Karl enjoyed the company of a friend, not even those friends he had grown up with in Lippaiken. He even did the unthinkable for a theology graduate: he unloosened his neckscarf, and by sunrise, like his host, his shirt was hanging loose over his pants and his boots had been kicked sideways beside the door. The two parted with warm words, vowing to meet again soon.

Luis felt lighter, energetic, free of pain. Fortunately, his body had the good sense to let him lapse into a deep sleep that lasted until midday.

Karl Amenda, too, was beside himself. Initially awed by the sheer weight carried by the name of the great Beethoven, he had relaxed into a comfortable relationship with the man so many called a terror.

"What a dear man, Henry," he later told Mylich, a guitarist who had been friends with Amenda since childhood. "You would never believe a more amiable person existed!"

It was in this mood (and Amenda always was in a good mood) that he met Mr. Hofrath as he walked to the Mozarts' home.

"Amenda!" Hofrath called. "How did you do it?"

"Do what, sir?" the musician asked.

"You have captured Beethoven's heart!" Hofrath exclaimed.

"Is that so rare?" Amenda asked. "He is so good and noble, how could not everyone adore him?"

Hofrath just laughed. "A minority opinion, I assure you!" he said, tipped his hat, and went on his way.

The late spring day seemed extraordinary. In every square, riots of colorful flowers, baskets of greens, mothers with squealing children, caparisoned horses in regal finery passing work horses pulling loads of merchandise to the business district around St. Stephan's. As winter boots were replaced with lightweight footwear, the rough cobblestones took their toll on many older pedestrians. But spirits were light, and even the church bells seemed to have a brighter timbre, almost tinkling in the mild air.

The darkness of the past few months had fallen from Luis's heart. He threw open the windows of his flat one bright morning and laughed loud and long, drawing some peculiar glances from passers-by, but what did he care? Music flowed again, easily and passionately, in his heart and mind. Five piano sonatas including the stormy *Pathetique*, three sonatas for violin, development of ideas in his first major orchestral works, all precedent-setting masterworks noted for their originality, passion, fire, and artistry. He could hardly keep up with the flow of ideas.

After shaving and ignoring the breakfast brought in by the cook herself, Luis sat down at the piano and considered a form he had yet to master: the string quartet. Some new melodies appeared, but how to elaborate on them, how to make them amount to something? He would study with Forster (no relation to the naturalist); Haydn said the time would come when he would need this world-class expert in the string quartet. And then he thought of his new friend, smiled, and improvised some variations on one of the morning's fresh melodies.

"Amenda, bring your friend the guitarist over tomorrow, that is an instrument I would like to know more about," said Luis, as the two walked through the city enjoying the mild air. The two now were so inseparable that acquaintances remarked that if you saw one of the men alone, you would have to ask, "Where is the other?"

"I'll do that, Beethoven," said Amenda, who seldom called his friend by his first name, and finally assented to use the last only after being soundly scolded for calling him Master. "You do not call your friends 'Master'!" the composer had insisted. "Indeed, where the violin is concerned, it is you, not I who deserves the title of Maestro."

Mylich had mixed feelings, however, when Amenda proposed the meeting. Mylich was an interesting character, also in his mid-20s, with sandy blond hair and a short beard. He was about Luis's height, but heavier, and wore a tan coat and broad-rimmed hat, giving him the uniform coloring of winter wheat. He had a suspicious streak, and would narrow his pale amber eyes if he thought there was trouble afoot. And did so as Amenda effused about the proposed meeting.

The two men had traveled in France, keeping a low profile during the unrest, and living on their earnings as musicians and itinerant teachers since Amenda had graduated from Jena two years before. While friends from childhood, there was no strong emotional connection between the two men, but Mylich was frankly envious to see his colleague swept up in such a sudden intense affection.

"Why should I?" Mylich groused, tightening the pegs on his guitar. "I have some music by Doisy to work on. This Beethoven doesn't care about guitar music. He probably just wants to examine me like a lab specimen!"

"Honestly," said the amiable Amenda with a laugh, "he is nothing like that! You've heard all the rumors about his temper, but in reality, he a sweet-tempered creature. At least with me."

Mylich smiled bitterly. Yes, his friend was lost. Perhaps he was even in love! "I suppose it wouldn't hurt," he added at last, "at least I can tell people in the future that I gave guitar lessons to the great pianist Beethoven!"

The two friends arrived at Luis's flat the following afternoon, to the sound of very loud piano practice, even to the degree of pounding. They looked at each other, even Amenda a bit puzzled, but knocked on the door, and there being no answer, went inside. Since the piano was facing the door, Luis saw them as they entered, and put down his work.

"Amenda! And you must be Mylich! Come over here, oh, I can't offer you anything to drink, this is the servant's day off."

Mylich put his guitar case on a bench near the entrance, and shook Luis's hand.

"My friend," said Amenda to Luis, "whatever were you playing? And why so loud?" Luis's back was toward Amenda at this point, and he did not respond. Amenda put his hand on Luis's shoulder, and asked again, this time face to face.

"Oh, nothing, really, just testing the dynamics of the instrument. So, Mylich, let me see this wonder: a six-stringed guitar! And they say there is nothing new under the sun!"

Mylich opened the case and proudly produced his one treasure, a gleaming golden instrument that further matched his own coloring.

"May I?" he asked, carrying it to an armless chair. Amenda fetched a footstool and put it at his friend's feet.

"Yes, play me something," said Luis, "play several pieces, I want to hear the range."

Amenda went to the piano and pressed the E and A keys in sequence, and Mylich spent a short time in tweaking the pitch.

"First," the guitarist said to Luis, "something by Moretti, then an etude by Pollet. And I have a surprise!" he said with a half-smile to Amenda, who raised an eyebrow in curiosity.

Now Mylich was a skillful musician, who also played violin and viola, but this was not yet the era of the classical guitar. That would not come for another decade or so, and in fact, Beethoven would become part of its culture and lore when he befriended the great guitarist Giuliani some 15 years later. But at this time and place, the guitar was emerging from the shadows of its reputation as a popular musical accessory of little value into a new age as a concert instrument to be reckoned with. Mylich and others whom history has forgotten were the standard-bearers who exploited the potential of the new six-stringed guitar and collected and performed the works of now forgotten composers for this instrument. On these foundations, the great masters of guitar music— Carcassi, Carulli, Giuliani, and above all others, Sor—would build an enduring legacy.

The sonority of the guitar filled the room. At first, Amenda listened wholeheartedly to his friend's performance, then his eyes fell on Luis, whose expression was uncharacteristically fixed, with little change of expression. However, when Mylich's playing was more forceful and dynamic, Luis's features brightened, and he nodded in time with the instrument's rhythm. This puzzled Amenda, and he made a mental note to mention it later in private.

The guitar is a very romantic instrument, suggesting warm, exotic climates, unlocking the secrets of the heart, arousing deep emotions, soothing and dispelling cares. Mylich's sensitive, expressive performance lulled the listeners into a kind of hypnotic state as they sat together across the room. A less experienced audience might have fallen asleep, but each cadence awakened a subtle turn of mind in these two friends who listened with such profound appreciation, attention, and pleasure.

"And now one final piece," said Mylich, adding, "I found the score, Amenda, among your things. I realize it has not yet been published." He smiled ambiguously.

Then, Mylich tightened the pegs a bit more, checked the pitch, and sat down with his leg elevated on the footstool. He then began to play his transcription of the famous slow movement of the Pathetique Sonata.

Amenda's jaw dropped, and though it took a few measures for Luis to understand what was happening, he soon sat upright in his chair, his eyes large and burning, first with a bit of confusion, perhaps a sense of betrayal, even outrage, but then, as always, the music won. Mylich's performance of this haunting, sublime music, only recently released from the composer's brain, won over both friends, and by the end, tears glistened in the Master's eyes. Without a word, he rose and ran to the guitarist, crushing him in a hug with the guitar pressed precariously between them, saying nothing, but breathing heavily.

And at last he said, "I forgive you, Mylich. No one else could steal my work still unpublished and win my heart. I wish I had composed that for guitar! The guitar: it is an entire orchestra in your hands."

And so it was that Mylich became an occasional visitor to the Beethoven flat and even taught Luis the fundamentals of the instrument, though he never did compose specifically for the guitar.

Chapter 13

Despite loss and occasional ill health, these final years of the eighteenth century were for Luis some of his happiest. His friendship with Amenda, the growing public adulation of his musicianship, even the extreme reception of his original compositions, which aroused as much outrage as ecstasy: all these contributed to his already high level of self confidence and eagerness to rise to the top of his profession.

But it cannot be overemphasized just how many obstacles this still-young man had to overcome in terms of resistance to his physical appearance, foreign accent, and cock-sure attitude. With the ban on Freemasonry and other societies a decade earlier and the cultural shift from an intellect-based Enlightenment to a feelings-based Romanticism, scholars who once wrote eloquently about the equality of all people fell into disregard. Without the moderating effect of these high-level intellectual societies, opinions superseded facts, and personal vanity overtook objectivity.

Junk science, perpetrated by the highly unreliable scholars Meiners and Spittler, fed the narcissism of Austrian and Germanic society. Interestingly, both men had been members of the radical Illuminati. When that organization was crushed, they took their viewpoint (shared by few within the brotherhood) and marketed it aggressively to the white upper class, which was looking for affirmation and stability in an age of Revolution. A widespread view in which human types were prioritized according to how closely they looked like the Germanic aristocracy began to emerge.

This ideal race, modeled after prototypes studied in the mountains outlying Russia, even had a name. Blumenbach called it "Caucasian." Soon, the feelings-besotted Viennese were redefining beauty as the fairest of the fair. Meiners, relying on old travelogues rather than scientific inquiry, went so far as to identify two races: the beautiful (i.e., European) and the ugly (everyone else). It was in this climate of racial divisiveness that the Natural History Museum confiscated the remains of Angelo Soliman and stuffed him like a hunting trophy.

Where did Luis fit in all this? He was probably too busy with music to pay much attention, but others were watching him, and often with displeasure. It was a culture in which, increasingly, ugly meant black, and black meant bad or inferior. There was no way around it. Writer after writer recorded reactions to Beethoven when he played in public or when individuals encountered him on the street.

"He is a short, ugly, dark, cross-looking young man," groused the pianist Gelinek. "He had a shock of jet black hair…(and)…a beard of several days' growth (which) made his naturally dark face still blacker," wrote the pedagogue Carl Czerny who, as a child, first met the composer in 1801.

Spurning his proposal of marriage a few years earlier, the singer Magdalina Willmann called him "ugly and half mad." The wife of the Bonn baker Fischer, in whose house the Beethovens once lived, recalled Luis as, "short and stocky, broad-shouldered, with a short neck, large head, round nose and swarthy complexion; he always stooped forward when walking. At home, even as a young man, he was called *the Spaniard*."

The steadying influence of the Freemasons and Illuminati had all but disappeared from the German-speaking world, and the void left by rational science had been filled with irrational prejudice and self-love. Luis's achievement in rising to the top of musical society as a young adult is all the more remarkable when the obstacles of intolerance and the worship of Aryan appearances are taken into account.

For Amenda, though, Luis's appearance was never an issue. He loved the Master heart and soul, as a comrade and companion. But visiting the composer's chaotic apartment caused him to wonder whether there was anything he could do to make the Master's life and work easier.

One morning as Amenda and Luis's brother Carl, who was serving as a kind of unpaid secretary, were going through some business papers while Luis worked on his compositions in the next room, the two heard a loud shout and the sound of everything being swept off the piano in a single blow and sent crashing or rustling to the floor, then the roaring discord of a body falling onto the keys. The two men rushed in, to find Luis in complete disarray sitting on the bench.

"I can't find it! I can't find my sketches! How can I work like this? I left them right…*here*!" A powerful hand crashed down on the small side table. Luis was in the habit of writing musical ideas on single sheets of paper, which would flutter behind the cabinet, into the trash, or turn up as the servant's idea of an impromptu liner for a breakfast tray.

"I have an idea," whispered Karl Amenda to Carl, as the latter helped his brother look for the missing sheet. Karl's idea was a simple one, though simple solutions are usually the last to be developed. The next day, Amenda arrived at the studio and handed the surprised composer a package, neatly wrapped in brown paper and tied with string.

"Amenda, my dearest, what is this? Not my name day, is it an anniversary of some sort?" He picked up a greasy knife, cut the string, and hastily opened the present, letting the wrapping fall to the floor. Inside was a simple notebook.

Still smiling, but as baffled as before, Luis glanced up at Amenda. "And…?" he asked, looking back at the notebook and flipping through its large blank pages.

"It's a sketchbook!" said Karl in his usual pleasant, helpful manner. "Luis, it's for your new quartets! You won't lose the sketches if you write them in this book: they will be right there for you, now and forever!" Luis sat on the edge of the piano bench, and rubbed his chin between his thumb and forefinger, the way he did when he was considering a new idea. Amenda was on pins and needles, fearing the book would go flying across the room.

But Luis threw his head back and laughed amiably. "Brilliant!" he said. "Why didn't I think of this. Here," he thrust the book and pencil at Amenda, "you copy out these for starters…" and then thrust a wad of single sheets at his companion.

"Oh, no," said Karl, backing up, "this is your project! Entirely your work, Beethoven!"

Luis wrinkled his nose at the thought of the drudgery of copying. "Then, I'll simply start from fresh! Come on, let's go out for coffee," he said, and the two men left the chaos for the orderly world of Viennese commerce.

The sketchbook proved a godsend, and set Luis on a more orderly path of organizing his thoughts, which actually influenced the way he conceived and developed musical ideas. Once again, his new best friend had proven that he knew Luis better than Luis knew himself. The warm season was coming to an end, however, and more engagements, study, and even the prospect of a long trip loomed in the months ahead.

"Amenda," said Luis, one day as they strolled in the Schoenbrunn Park, "you are…an angel!" Karl blushed looked down as they walked. "No, come here, see this big low branch? I like to come here and think through my musical ideas. And see, I have a sketchbook with me!" he added, pulling it from under his light jacket. Amenda nodded approvingly. "No, sit here. Karl, I think sometimes you were sent to me by a benevolent Creator to keep me out of trouble. You know me so well, it's as though you looked into my very soul."

"You are a person of great depth," said Amenda simply, "more than you understand, perhaps, and certainly more than others perceive. The public, they view you as a magician, an entertainer who can startle them with superhuman feats of virtuosity, and shock their ears with dissonance and novelty."

Luis nodded, enjoying the affirmation of his own assessment. "You are a spiritual genius, Amenda," he said, laying his hand on his friend's shoulder. "Some day, you might make a great pastor, but Karl." He tightened his grip on his friend. "Karl, do not leave me. How I have longed for someone who understands me and who cherishes the same ideals that I do, someone to share my life."

Amenda looked into Luis's eyes with concern as well as feeling. "It is God's way that men should marry," he said, "but you are right: where would you find such a woman? Someone who was your equal in mind and body, but also tender-hearted enough to take care of you, organize your life, and share your dreams."

Luis was silent for a while, and his hand fell to his side. "I knew such a woman, a girl, actually, many years ago," he said, looking out into the distance. "No," he said, "I may yet *love* another woman, but there is only one person, at this moment, I feel I could share my life with, and that is quite a different matter." He looked at Karl with an almost painful feeling of affection and attachment. Amenda took his friend's hand, and held it for some time. Neither spoke, and somehow the long day ended at last. Before long, the cooler weather set in, and Luis was dispatched on a concert tour in Prague, while Amenda continued teaching and performing in the Lobkowitz Court and at the Mozart home.

In Prague that Fall, Luis made an indelible impression on an international audience. Not only was he heralded as a great pianist, perhaps without equal, but for the first time he was celebrated as the greatest new composer on the musical scene.

He gave two public concerts in the Convictsaale, a concert hall. The first, performed before a large audience, consisted of the C major piano concerto, movements from the A major Sonata op. 2 no. 2, and a brilliant improvisation on an air by Mozart. Later, the pianist and composer Tomaschek, who attended the concert, wrote, "Beethoven's magnificent playing, and especially his bold improvisation, made such a revolution in my thoughts and feelings, that *for several days I did not touch the piano.*"

His income bolstered significantly by the enterprise, Luis bid farewell to Prague, with its statue-lined Charles Bridge, glittering church spires, and medieval town square, and returned to Vienna in early November. There he returned to his third-floor flat and worked diligently on the work that would become his third String Quartet, while studying Italian vocal writing with Salieri, the master of Italian opera in Vienna, at the court music hall. A whirlwind of activities, concerts, pleasantries with the Prince and Princess, parties, more composing, kept the young master from seeing his dearest friend more than a few times.

"We will get together, I promise you," whispered Luis, escorting Amenda to the door as a publisher arrived with a proposal. "Our time is drawing near! I have so much to do!" Amenda embraced him tenderly. "I know," he said. "I will do anything for you. Even wait."

The New Year—and the beginning of a new century—was scarcely noticed by the preoccupied composer. His health was not at its best, and the buzzing in his ears had sent him to a doctor and occasionally out of town to a spa in search of a remedy, which was not forthcoming. The next string quartet, delineated in the sketchbook, was put on the back burner as Luis worked on a new set of variations on a theme by his teacher, Salieri. The Italian was always on his mind, as nothing could be as important to the Viennese music-loving public as opera, a compositional field in which Luis had little experience though he grew up playing the viola parts of all the latest operas in the Bonn court orchestra. Salieri, variations, the string quartets, then the publication of his violin sonatas, dedicated to Salieri as well, gave the young composer little rest. The world beyond his apartment in the Lichnowsky Palace quaked before the encroaching armies of Napoleon, who had conquered Egypt and now seemed unstoppable as he pushed to the east, crossing into Syria and on to Gaza.

Despite an intense dislike, perhaps even loathing of teaching, Luis was persuaded to indulge his benefactor, the Countess Anna Brunsvik, by taking on her two daughters as piano students. As it turned out, the young ladies, Therese who was about 24, and Josephine, 20, were beautiful and cultured as well as talented. That spring, composition and daily walks with Amenda both came to a screeching standstill: Luis was lost in the charms of two highly alluring ladies of high status, once again triggering the fantasy that the "van" in his name signified royalty, and that, perhaps, he might indeed have been the unacknowledged love child of the King of Prussia.

He visited the two sisters at The Golden Gryphon every day at 1 o'clock sharp for an hour-long lesson that soon lengthened into two, three, sometimes four hours or more. Luis was smitten, and they seemed to dote on him, devouring every word he spoke, tolerating his peculiar, un-Viennese appearance, from his swarthy complexion and untamed hair, down to his unconventional but warm leggings made of shaggy black goat hair. What giggles transpired behind his back, he mercifully did not know. All he saw were wealthy proto-countesses drinking in his every word, and performing for him like prize peacocks at his every command and whim.

The intense studies, which overshadowed every other occupation of his life and gave the bored girls something to do and later to gossip about, had two positive outcomes. First, it enabled Luis to develop his original technique for playing and teaching the piano, which involved playing with bent fingers, almost claw-like hands, perched over the keys, rather than the flat-handed approach which had prevailed. This allowed a powerful attack, a song-like legato, both indispensible in the performance of Luis's own music.

Second, despite the frivolity, the banter, the heavy-handed joking that caused the young women to titter behind their hands, it also helped Luis develop a teaching style which would benefit many other students in the years ahead (such as Carl Czerny and Ferdinand Ries).

The Prince reached out to Amenda, and Amenda reached out to Albrechtsberger and Schenk, and other friends and teachers, but no one could devise a diversion to extract Luis from his obsessive attachment to the gifted Brunsvik sisters, which was doing absolutely nothing to advance his compositional technique and output, nor sustain his reputation as a recitalist.

His life seemed a series of unplanned detours. Indeed, the pleasures of the year—the stimulating rapport with Salieri, the full-time occupation of entertaining the Brunsvik sisters, and a piano duel with a good-natured musician named Wölffl— all were transitory interludes in a life that was soon to be shaken to the core.

Chapter 14

The Brunsvik sisters had moved on. In fact, Josephine was married that spring to a Count she did not love, while Therese remained with her mother. Luis was once again alone, and, looking up one morning, realized Amenda was missing from his life.

Amenda! Where was the beloved friend, the fellow musician who shared the birth of so many of his recent works, the noble colleague who shared his passion for immortal works of literature and wisdom?

"Amenda, Amenda, where have you been?" cried Luis to no one in particular, and without jacket or hat, bounded down the stairs and briskly walked to Amenda's flat. Their talk at the Schoenbrunn came back to him, he could almost hear the words ringing within his head. The follies of the past few weeks nearly filled him with shame, though he really did enjoy them at the time. He walked faster, the early June sun warming his face, until he arrived at his friend's apartment. How wonderful when we join our domestic arrangements, he thought, looking up at the window where he half expected to see the tall silhouette of Karl playing the violin. Ever mine…ever thine…

The door opened and a disheveled Mylich appeared, none too happy to see his friend's idol. "Sir, we haven't seen or heard of you in some time," he said, with a yawn. It was definitely too early for a guitarist to be up and about.

"I must see Amenda! Let me in," said Luis impatiently, almost shoving Mylich aside.

"Sir, wait," he said, grabbing Luis's arm. "He's not here, he had to meet his uncle."

"Why, is something wrong?" Luis spun around. "What is it?"

Mylich sighed. While recognizing the greatness of his guest, and admiring him as a musician and composer, Mylich had often reflected of late how his good friend from childhood had all but been abandoned by a beloved companion. Luis could see it in Mylich's eyes.

"I've been busy, very busy," he mumbled. "Tell me, where is he, what is wrong?"

"You know that Karl is the second son of his family," Mylich said cautiously.

"Yes, yes, what of it?" Luis was becoming impatient.

"Well, it's his older brother. He has passed away, in an accident."

"Oh!" Luis put out an arm to brace himself against the doorframe. "Oh, poor Karl! I am so sorry! How horrible!"

Mylich waited a moment. "He is very upset, yes. Perhaps you should leave him alone during this time…"

"Alone! I can do no such thing!" exclaimed Luis. "I need him! He must see me, where did you say he is?"

"I didn't," said Mylich, developing a cold tone. He noticed how Luis said he needed Karl, but did not suggest that it was Karl who may have needed comforting. "Sir," said Mylich, "I am not sure where he is, he was vague on that score. But he should return in a few days. I suspect he will have to travel home."

"Home!" Luis was beside himself. "To Latvia?"

Mylich nodded. "Sir," he said, "I really need to leave you now. Why don't you write a note to Karl and send it here by post. He will be sure to see it first thing when he returns."

Luis hardly knew what to do. His brain was pulled in several different directions, his feet didn't know whether to run back home, or take him to one of his teachers or patrons. No, the latter would not do, since what he needed now was a friend, someone he could confide in, and his two best friends in the world—the late Lorenz von Breuning and the soon-to-depart Karl Amenda—were conspicuously unavailable. There was no one. No one to talk to, from whom to seek advice or consolation or reassurance. He walked briskly to the park, but unable to find solace even in nature, moved on to a coffee shop to sharpen his wits. Back at the flat, the caffeine made his normally undecipherable scrawl even less intelligible, but he wrote the note, and began searching through his papers for music that would memorialize the occasion.

A week later, there was a rap at his door, and the servant admitted Karl. He looked care-worn, but in his rush to embrace him, Luis saw only the tender glow of inner beauty, peacefulness, and affection. The two men stood in this embrace for some time, Luis with his head against Karl's chest, as though at the same time feeling and listening to his heartbeat. The servant rolled her eyes, and left the room muttering to herself, thinking once again of finding a new position. Luis took Karl's hand and led him to a divan, pushed some papers and dirty clothes onto the floor, knocking over a wine flask with his foot, and then the two men sat.

"You've heard," said Karl, in his kind, melodious voice.

Luis grimaced and shook his head. "Is there any way around this?" he asked. "Surely, the funeral is past."

Karl was silent for a moment. "It is not about the funeral," he said. "John was the first-born son. Now, that role has fallen to me. In the hierarchy of the family, it is time for me to come home and take my place."

Luis nodded in understanding. He himself was the first-born son and since a young age had accepted that responsibility fully and enthusiastically. For this new era was not only the age of feeling and romance, it was also the age of nobility and heroism, and one needed to be honorable within one's own family before one could pretend to lead in the larger world.

"I know," he said softly, with a note of resignation. Resignation: that was a new concept to him, but one that appeared time and again in the writings of the Stoic masters whose ancient words he had taken to heart.

Karl paused again for some moments. "It will not be a short-term absence," he said. "I fear…or rather, know…that the time of my wandering must end. I need to assume my work in my community, support and lead my family, take on the duties of pastor for which I was educated. In time," he added, more softly, "I will marry, a pastor must. All this will be a memory, a dream.

"However," he turned Luis's face toward his own, "my dearest beloved, I don't know how I can leave you." Tears shone in his pale blue eyes, and Luis tightened his grip on both his hands.

Luis was unable to contain the emotion that swept through him. "We are one Soul within two bodies," he said. "How can that Soul be divided? We will always be together through time, through space…"

"I wish it were so, I wish to God it were so," said Karl, his hands falling into the strong grip of his friend. "Silent love," he said, and Luis's brow furrowed.

"What do you mean?" he asked.

"I was thinking of Boehme, the Protestant mystic. He was my favorite writer when I was at Jena. I never really cared for Luther, you know. Boehme said, '*Heaven is nothing other than a revelation of the Eternal One, where everything works and wills in silent love.*'"

Luis said nothing, but the impact of these words touched his heart and mind profoundly. It was so different from the declarations of priests and princes and generals, the huge Bureaucracy of Meaning that tried to tell people how to act, think, feel, what societies they could or could not belong to; how to live, die, even compose. Certainly, Luis had encountered some supernatural presence—call it God if you must—within music throughout his entire life. He remembered watching the hills from River Street in Bonn and the ecstasy of Nature during his childhood years, and the feeling of both mastery and utter surrender he experienced when improvising brilliantly before a large audience.

"That is your gift to me," said Luis. "I, too, have a gift for you, something similar. Let me package it up and send it to you, for you must be on your way."

Before Karl left, Luis said, "I must know for certain that some time in the future—even if it is the very distant future—we will meet again."

"I cannot say…" murmured Amenda, "my life is so uncertain now, there will be so many changes…"

"A dozen years, then!" cried Luis, clapping his hands on his friend's arms. "Hopefully sooner, but assuredly, if we are both alive, we can add this distant date to our calendars and build our lives toward that reunion if no other."

Karl nodded, improbable though the idea was. "Fine, but it seems too long. The world is too unsettled a place."

"It will not be the first time, I am certain! We will meet many times again, and perhaps I can persuade you to bring your ministry to Vienna!" said Luis with a wink. But Karl's smile was sad.

"Summer, then, July…1812…but where?"

"Karlsbad," quipped Luis, "in your honor." Karl nodded, and the two exchanged a Masonic-type handshake, and embraced one final time.

"I will live for that day," said Luis, as Karl, out of ear-shot, walked briskly down Petersplatz, and turned a corner. How would he know that both would in fact live to and beyond that date, but they would not meet again on that day or ever again?

In a few weeks, already on his long journey home, Karl received a package from Luis. It contained a copy of the Quartet in F (op. 18, no. 1). The note read,

"Dear *Amenda!* take this quartet as a small memento of our friendship, (and) whenever you play it recall the days which we passed together and the sincere affection felt for you then and which will always be felt by, your warm and true friend…

"Farewell, dear A., and give me news, soon, of your stays en route and also when you have arrived back in your homeland." Luis's sketchbook revealed that the second movement, haunting and heartbreaking in its tenderness, unlike any expression of pathos and yearning yet captured in music, was meant to convey the feelings expressed in the tomb scene of Shakespeare's *Romeo and Juliet.* It was as though he knew that the greatest love would end, but not in silence.

Chapter 15

In the final months of the year, Luis threw himself into his work. The great Septet, more variations, the publication of two of the Piano Sonatas. How could Mozart have composed his three greatest symphonies in a single summer! The man must have been bewitched. In actuality, it was just a matter of the diverse ways in which the brains of creative people work. For Luis, composing was more than inspiration alone: it required an architect's attention to foundations and structure, to create a framework within which inspiration could be released on an unprecedented scale.

And during this time, and the months to follow in the new century, Luis transformed the idea of the four-movement symphony pioneered by Haydn. Under Luis's masterful hand the symphony as a whole became like a cohesive novel in four connected chapters, sweeping toward an astonishing conclusion.

To achieve this transformation, he had to dissect and rearrange section after section, taking the finale from the first movement, moving it to the end of the fourth, and rebuilding the structure brick by brick, chapter by chapter, depending on which metaphor you choose to apply. And on top of that, he started the work in a foreign key, something that had not been done before. He smiled: that would set the critics on their ear!

There were more concerts and recitals through the end of the year and into the new, and Luis wisely dedicated a work to the wife of the court theater director, increasing his chances of snagging a coveted reservation at the Burgtheater in the spring. And snag it he did for on April 2, Luis had the theater to himself for the mounting of his first grand public concert.

The program included works by Mozart and Haydn, but featured the premier of the First Symphony, whose opening chords in a foreign key brought gasps from the large audience, as well as one of his piano concertos and some freeform improvisation. While the critics carped about the orchestra's playing, perhaps they were too dumbfounded to find the words to describe the miraculous transformation of symphonic form developed by the still young composer.

In addition to his success as a pianist and composer, Luis's star was on the rise in terms of income. His patron, Prince Lichnowsky, gave him a generous annuity so he could focus on his compositions. In addition, other patrons eagerly commissioned works and paid handsomely for dedications (though not all dedications were "bought").

Shortly after the public concert, Luis met the great hornist Punto, an international superstar on his instrument, who was traveling through Vienna. Born in Bohemia, the son of a serf, Punto made a stunning reputation for himself as a musician and a bit of a wastrel. The composer promised the spirited musician a new sonata, and a date and venue for its premier had been set. However, between the public concert and other obligations, Luis did not have a chance to *begin* composing the sonata until the day before it was to be premiered. For a man who took nearly four years to compose a symphony, this was rushing it a bit, but he worked through the night, and Punto and he debuted the work as scheduled, to great acclaim. "I will never do that again," swore Luis, mopping his brow, after the recital. But, of course, he did.

Despite the rough start, Punto and Luis hit it off, and Luis was quite knowledgeable about the horn as an instrument, thanks to his association as a young man with Simrock, the Bonn hornist, publisher, and Illuminati brother. They agreed to take the sonata on the road the following month. But in the meantime, a new wrinkle emerged in the life of musical Vienna, this time involving Luis's growing faction of enemies.

Daniel Steibelt had been spreading rumors about Luis. Acknowledged as a major pianist of the era, Steibelt was a tall, proud dandy with an aggressive Prussian air. He also had a reputation for underhanded dealings and manipulating people and rules to his own advantage. He arrived in Vienna one afternoon, and some say it was for one reason only: to challenge "that hack Beethoven" to a piano competition.

Though a bit overworked, basking in the afterglow of his first public concert, and the successful completion and performance of the Horn Sonata, Luis had seldom felt better. In this spirit, he accepted an invitation to play on the same program as Steibelt at the home of Count von Fries. Each musician performed an original work, to the satisfaction of a large assortment of guests, including those in each composer's camp. Luis played the piano in a performance of his own Clarinet Trio (Opus 11), and there were no exchanges of fire at this first meeting.

The second meeting, a week later, was an entirely different story. This was a true competition, divided into three rounds, providing plenty of fireworks for an even larger audience. After Steibelt had competently played the piano part in one of his quintets, he did something especially snarky. He took a theme from a recent work by Luis and then wove a series of what he thought were superior variations on the purloined tune. In the context of the time, this was a slap in the face to Beethoven, and Luis felt it physically as though it were an actual blow.

Throughout the variations, accompanied by coos of approval in the rival camp, Luis sat silently, his arms across his chest, jaw tight, muscles taut, eyes blazing as they almost burned holes in the Prussian's natty serge. After the performance and roars of applause (from one section of the audience) were over, Luis just sat there, still glaring.

The room grew very quiet. Then he rose slowly, and walked over to the cellist's chair, roughly snatching the cello part from Steibelt's Quintet, scrunching it in his hand. Then he smoothed it out, held it up, like a sleight-of-hand artist, for the audience to see, and turned it upside down. He smashed it against the piano music stand, sat down on the bench with a thud, and proceeded to pound the theme upside down *and backwards* in a mocking tone, and then improvised the most astonishing set of variations, at every conceivable tempo, register, and mood, from this scrap of mangled music, until the audience rose before he was done and screamed and shouted in complete surrender.

Before Luis had even finished playing, Steibelt stormed out of the room in a fury, left the house, and indeed left Vienna *never to return.* And so it was that Luis was once again the conquering hero. With that display, Luis completed his life as a competitive pianist, and there would be no more duels. He was the undisputed King of the Piano, and challengers would no longer come knocking at his door.

After perhaps the busiest month in his life to date, there was no down time for Luis. In May, Punto and he traveled to nearby Hungary for a short tour, after the first recital, the two got into a heated argument at dinner about articulation, and before long, Punto was rising to his feet and shouting, and Luis was breaking china, and the inn-owner was beside himself. Punto threw down his napkin and stomped out of the inn, leaving Luis to angrily throw some extra coins on the table to cover the damages and to storm back to his room.

While Punto went on to other cities alone, Luis stayed in Pest for nearly three months, making connections, networking, playing short recitals, writing in his sketchbooks. It was here, in the quiet on the outskirts of the beautiful small city, that he decided to add some organization to his own life, not simply to ride the currents of demand as he had done this year, but to put the kind of structure he had built in the First Symphony into his own existence. For a letter had been forwarded to him from Amenda which put an end to one cherished dream and would require him to pursue other paths to personal happiness.

Chapter 16

Luis took the letter to a window seat. This part of the room was flooded with late afternoon light, especially luminous in this foreign land, so flat and open and devoid of tall buildings. He unfolded the letter, smoothed it out on his lap, and read:

"My Beethoven.

"I still approach you with the same sincere love and respect that the value of your heart and of your talent irresistibly demand of me and eternally will demand of me.

"You might ask how I could withhold, at least this reassurance, from you for so long? Dear one, o! rather ask: *how could I only leave you?*

"…See*, beloved! that is how I think of my relationship with you*. Only this conviction can explain to me the beginning and continuance of our ties. These statements might seem too flattering and enthusiastic to you; I am not able to express these things more strongly and distinctly. However, you must not be wrong about this: *You are no ordinary human being!* Whoever knows you as I do and only loves you in a common way, I do not consider him worthy of the divine feeling of love.

"However, where *will I find my longing, now?* Here in rough Latvia…wherever one knows me, there also lives Beethoven's name. Some play your piano pieces with pleasure, particularly Mylich's sister. (She and the old father) now want to hear nothing but of Beethoven. It is my sweetest musical enjoyment, when she plays for me. Then I often forget myself and, with your heavenly harmonies, believe to hear *my* Beethoven, himself. *Then the fiery feelings awaken in me, with which your company inspired me, in the liveliest manner; then I feel as if I have to get away from here, **to you, to the source of my most tender and liveliest feelings**. Oh, why did my fate ask so much sacrifice of me!*

"However, my fate is, perhaps, already sealed, I might be tied down here, forever," Amenda lamented. "A beautiful, young, talented girl from Geneva who is being raised in the same noble house in which I spent several happy years, has captured your Amenda…my heart had to warm up here, too, and *totally submit*," he wrote, clearly with resignation rather than happiness, "to the subject…I only live two miles away from this girl."

Ah, thought Luis, an unavoidable obligation!

"I am more conscientious in fulfilling my duties than I was in Vienna…O! now I regret all hours that I spent too little in your company; and the memory of that which I experienced, of your friendship, of your art—my dearest, this (memory) shall still be the most pleasant (of all my memories) in the hour of my death.

"O my Beethoven! never forget a friend who, although perhaps separated from you, *forever, will do everything to become more worthy of your love. You still fill my entire heart*…Wherever you are, beloved! my longing is following you. *With the loss of my well-being, I want to pay for yours*. Only tell where and how you live to your, eternally, *Karl A.*

Luis smoothed the paper gently, and his glance fell outside, on the fir trees and oaks, the patches of blue sky. He rested his head against the window, and tears of sadness and longing welled in his eyes. Clearly, Amenda was now a prisoner of responsibility: he must stay with his family, he must fulfill his vocation, he must marry—soon there would be reports of children. Their grand plan to live together—two idealistic musicians with no other ties, to travel perhaps to Italy or Poland, to live out their lives together as one—this plan was gone forever.

Perhaps they could stay in touch by post, virtual friends. Luis shook his head to himself—a sad alternative. More work, that always seemed the solution. He had his brothers to watch over; that would be *his* responsibility. And perhaps one of the fair maidens he tutored on the keyboard would consent to be a bride, especially nice if she brought a father's fortune with her. If not, no matter. "You are no ordinary man," wrote Amenda. Luis knew this. Perhaps it was his fate to be married to his art.

But something else changed in Luis's heart in these last days in Pest. He had been listening to the sounds of nature: birds, insects, wind. It might have been the lay of the land, but he could swear they were muted, not vivid as he last remembered them in his nature walks outside of Vienna.

Muted, and yet his illnesses had been at bay for some time. The pianos here were out of tune; they didn't have the strong resonance of the Viennese models. He would compare his memory of them with his own instruments when he returned home. He could not wait. He could not leave to get home fast enough.

Chapter 17

The Prince's own barber had worked on Luis's hair in preparation for the portrait session. "I never saw hair like this in my life!" exclaimed the barber. "I need a saw, not scissors." Luis paid him no heed. People were always complaining about or commenting on his unruly hair. Being a royal barber, the tradesman politely reserved any further comments, but later told stories to his colleagues about the most difficult mane he had ever tamed.

Luis, on the other hand, was uncharacteristically silent and introspective on his return from Hungary. How he hated having his portrait painted, and yet, that was par for the course with any successful author or composer. Publishers clamored for fresh images of their best sellers, which were engraved and often appeared along with scores or bound volumes.

Luis would be dressed impeccably and have to sit still for hours over several days. Well, it wasn't an entire loss of time. There seemed to be an endless stream of high-born ladies to flirt with. And the adoring Josephine attended his recitals whenever she could. His refined appearance would certainly win points with the ladies. But when Luis looked spiffy, you could be sure he was not composing.

And indeed he had much on his mind, which led him to pay Dr. Frank a visit in his office, rather than indulge in the house visits so common for those associated with the aristocracy. It was some time after the portrait had been completed that he met the doctor, who was director of the General Hospital. Dr. Frank was no stranger to Luis. The doctor's son, also a physician, had married Christina Gerhardi, one of Luis's most enthusiastic supporters in his early years in Vienna. Dr. Frank was a highly esteemed medical scholar as well as practitioner and administrator.

A lean man with an angular, sad face, Dr. Frank frowned and ran his hand over his thin hair. He then laid out his instruments neatly and examined the composer, whom he had visited before on other health matters. He referred to past notes about the buzzing in his patient's ears and his inability to detect high notes. The problem always cropped up when Luis had his frequent attacks of gastritis.

"You need to rest more, young man," the stern-looking physician said in his most imperious voice. "You are wearing yourself out. This business with your ears is nothing serious, but bears watching." He wrote some notes on a card and handed it to Luis. "Twice a day, warm oil in each ear. Stuff the passages with cotton. And the spas would be beneficial. Didn't you take advantage of the baths in Hungary? No? Too bad! See that you go back, or better yet, to Karlsbad, some of the better mineral springs." Well, mused Luis, I'll be there in 1812, but that is probably too late.

Luis was not convinced that Dr. Frank knew the seriousness of his problem, but it was a start, and the doctor was one of the most highly esteemed in Vienna. In the meantime, ignoring the medical advice, he returned to a busy world of composing, making final edits to the six quartets, more variations, and continuing to play brilliantly in the city's most fashionable salons. Composing was such hard work. Why couldn't music flow out of him as it did for Mozart? He was like a sculptor creating human forms from clay, hacking away at old material and then having to transpose parts from other works, sometimes turning a modeled foot into a hand, or a nose into an elbow. His sketchbook was filled with ink splatters, smudges, and ripped pages, a musical environment as disordered as his living quarters.

Luis thought often about Amenda, now settling down into domestic routine, and wished that fate, in the most idealized sense, for himself. The pretty girls of the aristocracy may have purred at his attention, but not one seriously considered him marriage material.

In January, while intently working on his Second Symphony, Luis accepted a commission to compose a ballet for *The Creatures of Prometheus*, a gaudy stage production, which nonetheless had a noble theme about the hero who sacrifices himself to bring great Art to humanity. It was exactly what he needed to establish himself as a versatile composer in tune with popular taste. The symphony was shelved for the time being, and Luis worked furiously on the ballet which was premiered in March, the ink still wet on the pages.

During this period, a new student appeared on the third floor of Greinersches Haus at 241 Tiefer Graben. One of Luis's great admirers and advocates, a musician named Krumpholz, introduced 10-year-old prodigy Carl Czerny to Luis. Luis had been many times to the Czerny home for musical get-togethers featuring musicians such as his old rival, Abbé Gelinek. A lad of average height and built, with a high broad forehead and wavy brown hair, Carl was not unknown to Luis. He had heard that the boy had even played a difficult Mozart concerto in public the year before and had been composing since the age of seven. Luis learned that the boy was very fond of new music and had begged his father to meet and study with the young master. Luis was flattered.

Krumpholz, the doting father Wenzel Czerny, and young Carl climbed the endless stairs up to Luis's flat, stopping several times for the elderly Krumpholz to catch his breath. Luis's current servant, a slovenly and downright dirty-looking man of middle age, led them into the master's messy music room, a chaos of scattered papers, articles of clothing, leftover food, with bare walls and only one rickety chair beside the excellent Walker piano. But the room was not bare of human company. A number of colleagues, including the violinist Schuppenzigh and brother Carl, awaited the child, whose heart beat faster at every step as he approached the forbidding nest. Soon, he was there, and Luis entered the room.

"(He) was dressed in a dark gray jacket and trousers of long dark goat's hair, which reminded me of the description of Robinson Crusoe I had just been reading," Czerny recalled years later. "Jet-black hair stood upright on his head. A beard, unshaven for several days, made his dark face even blacker...He had cotton wool, which seemed to have been dipped in some yellow fluid in both ears. His hands were covered with hair, and the fingers were very broad, especially at the tips."

This was a far cry from the matinee idol good looks of just a few years earlier. Luis nodded to his other guests, and looked fondly on the small boy. "What do you have to play?" he asked. Luis was short of stature, but must have seemed like a combination of Goliath and Methuselah to the youngster.

Carl said he would play the Mozart C Major concerto, which he did, and very well. With growing interest, Luis stood beside him to the left, and hunched over, his knee on the far end of the piano bench, as he played the accompaniment with his left hand, streaking the keys with a bit of ear oil left on his fingertips.

"Good work, boy," said Luis at last, then turning to the father. "I'll take him, he has talent. Send him here once a week." For sure, the lessons were less frequent than those given to the comely daughters of countesses, but they would be rigorous explorations of the pianist's art. And a good job he did of it, as Czerny later was to become the most renowned piano pedagogue in the German-speaking states and teacher of the incomparable Franz Liszt.

But still, Luis's friends and colleagues had no idea of the hearing loss that was failing to respond to treatment. Although satisfied with Frank as a general physician, Luis sought out specialists, as well as the physician Vering, who might be able to help his rapidly deteriorating hearing. On their advice, he took cold baths in the winter, warm baths in the Danube, herbal teas and ointments and pills, but nothing helped. The buzzing and humming grew louder until he clapped his hands over his ears and screamed.

Concurrently, he suffered from colic and diarrhea, not to mention the unbearable stress of pretense: always pretending he had no difficulties other than too much on his mind, always covering up the reason for his increasingly bad temper and dark moods, and ultimately, avoiding company altogether, a very difficult path for a celebrated pianist and much sought-after composer who moved in the highest circles of society.

By this time, though he hid it well, Luis had lost nearly 50 percent of his hearing.

Throughout the spring and following the triumph of his ballet, Luis continued a pathway that blended treatment with denial. On the one hand, he continued to see Dr. Frank regularly, to visit the baths in nearby towns, and to try any herbal treatment recommended by medicine or folklore. On the other hand, after a move to another part of the city, he threw himself into his work and evaded observations and questions by his Viennese friends, such as the good-natured Baron Zmeskall, with whom the composer exchanged outrageous puns and wordplay.

As summer approached, it brought with it one happy occasion for Luis: his good friend Stephan von Breuning, brother to Chris, Eleanor, and the late Lorenz, arrived in Vienna to join the civil service, and the move appeared permanent. The presence of an old Bonn friend, especially from the von Breuning clan, cheered him immensely. The serious, long-faced Stephan was not at all like his ebullient youngest brother, now deceased, but he was a true believer in Luis as a person and a creative genius, and was a limitless font of news from the old town, now suffering from the effects of war.

"You have no idea," Stephan lamented. "Nothing is the same."

But Luis wouldn't hear of it. "Napoleon has the right idea!" he insisted at their daily coffee klatsch. "The time has come for men and women to claim the freedom which is their birthright." Stephan would be quick to point out that no one benefited more from the conservative patronage system that Luis himself, but he would pooh-pooh the notion and insist that liberty was on the march. Just look at the former British Colonies, the Bastille! And how many innocent lives paid that price, Stephan reminded him. But their banter kept Luis's mind off of his own fears, and he was able to disguise his frequent requests that comments be repeated by using the excuse of absentmindedness. At least so he thought. Stephan was a sharp observer of human behavior, and it did not take him long to see that something serious was wrong with his childhood friend.

Another of his childhood companions, Wegeler, had stayed in Vienna only a short while and returned to Bonn as a physician and teacher. Once back in the small city, Wegeler found himself increasingly present at the von Breuning home, spending many hours with the mistress of the house and in the company of young Eleanor, who had grown into handsome spinsterhood. In fact, the physician, now approaching middle age himself, began to look upon this childhood friend in an entirely new light. Why hadn't this handsome, well-to-do, eligible woman married by now? What, or whom, was she waiting for?

It was at the von Breunings that Wegeler opened his mail on the last day in June. He opened Luis's letter while sitting in the parlor, flooded with sunlight, where they had so often discussed music and ideas with their dear friends and enlightened guests. It was indeed a long narrative, beginning with fond remembrances and pleasantries, but soon getting to the stark and horrible truth that he had not yet shared with another person:

"I am leading a wretched life. For two years, I have avoided all company, since it is not possible for me to say to people, 'I am deaf.' If I had been working in another field, it would still be better, but in my work, this is a terrible situation. Moreover, my enemies, whose number is not small, what would they say to this?

"In order to give you an idea of this peculiar deafness, I tell you that in the theater, I have to lean quite close to the orchestra in order to understand the actors. I do not hear the high notes of instruments and voices, and if I am a bit further away, I cannot hear anything…

"Often, I have cursed the Creator and my existence; Plutarch has taught me resignation, if that is possible in my situation. Otherwise, I will defy my fate. There will be moments in my life in which I will consider myself to be the most unhappy of God's creatures.

"I ask you not to tell anyone of my condition, not even <u>Lorchen</u> (Eleanor). *I am only confiding it to you as a secret…Resignation:* what a wretched refuge. And yet, it is the only one that is left to me…"

Wegeler was stunned, and barely noticed as Eleanor came into the room, and took the letter that he had placed beside him on the couch. Forgetting Luis's injunction not to tell her anything, Wegeler was lost in thought. But Eleanor read, tight-lipped, only her welling eyes revealing a passionate concern.

"Oh, Franz," she said, stifling a sob, "What are we going to do? You must help him!"

Wegeler shook his head. "I fear there is no help," he said. "We can only offer our friendship and support." He placed his hand on hers, and she sat beside him, her head on his shoulder, the tears silently falling.

Chapter 18

About a week later in Latvia, another friend was opening the mail, and smiled warmly to see the hand of his dearest friend on the envelope. Karl excused himself from his mother's presence, and quickly went up to his room. His heart was light, and a summer day had never been more glorious in the rough but pleasant countryside known as Courland.

Unlike his letter to Wegeler, Luis gushed right into an almost incoherent torrent of words about his deafness in a long stream of disjointed phrases, and the sensitive Amenda, fell back onto a chair as though he had just taken a blow to the chin.

"You are one of those whom my heart has chosen," he wrote, and again: "...I appeal to you to leave all else and come to me...You must be my companion!

"My heart beats as tenderly as ever for you," the impassioned narrative continued, "If by any chance I can serve you here, I need not say that you have only to command me."

Theological training may prepare one for clashes between God and man, but does little to protect the pastor from the greatest stirrings of his own heart. Amenda could not repress a cry, alerting the sharp ears of his mother who tapped on his door to ask what was wrong.

"It's all right, Mother," he said, trying to sound steady, "it's just a letter from a friend. I'll be all right. He had some disturbing news."

"All right, dear," the Mother's voice came through in a muffled way. "You need to have all your wits about you when we visit the Benoits later this morning. I am certain no fair lady wants a mawkish husband with red eyes!" He could hear her kindly laugh; she had a way of saying the most dreadful things in the most engaging manner.

Karl took a deep breath. His betrothal. The marriage. It would happen directly following his installation as pastor in Talsen. Jeanette was in love with him, and she truly was a dear girl, innocent and good. The families were completely in agreement, and the date was about to be set. And now this.

Karl took up the letter, wiped his eyes, blew his nose, and poured a glass of water. And to think they had spoken of meeting in a dozen years at the very latest. That would be too late. He would need to return to Vienna immediately. He would need to surrender everything: family, destiny, responsibility for the beloved who needed him so desperately. "And now these three remain: faith, hope and love," wrote the Apostle Paul. "But the greatest of these is love." That was the proof of love, to go to the beloved when needed regardless of circumstances.

Karl removed some writing paper from his table, and dipped his quill into the inkwell.

"My dearest Friend,

"How sweet your words are to me, yet how distraught I am over the news of your affliction. Have you no one to help you at this difficult time, no one who loves you and can at least attempt to ease a suffering I can barely imagine? Dearest One, let me be that person. No one loves you as I do, beloved Friend, and no one would be happier than to give up everything for you.

"My family here will do well without me, my presence here is a mere formality, and I have fulfilled my duty. As for my impending marriage, my heart is not in it, you know that. My ministry? What better vocation than loving and serving so great an Immortal Soul. That would be perfect happiness and my destiny.

"You must do this for me, and do it immediately: **send me an affirmation, a note, any sign** that you would welcome me to your home and that I could live with you, as a friend, an assistant, to help you find the best physicians, follow through with treatments, organize information, and even serve as your personal secretary. I know your brother is invaluable, but how much better to have two, including one whose love surpasses that of fraternal affection. I ask no income: I can resume my teaching, for I love the Mozart family and the Count assured me I would always be welcome.

"Dearest and sweetest of all Friends, true Beloved, reply to me, even a word on a scrap of paper will do, and I will leave immediately to be by your side. I will never leave you. And that is my solemn promise before God. I shall look for your reply each day. My life is entirely at your disposal and your command, and I can find no peace or happiness until I am with you.

"With most sincere affection and wishes for your recovery, Karl A"

Karl was trembling by the time he finished writing, with barely a drop of ink left in the inkwell. He placed the letter down for the ink to dry, and wrote Luis's summer address on the envelope, hoping his friend would not have moved again. When he had composed himself, Karl took the letter into town, a small settlement on the rough Latvian coast, and with a final moment gazing at the envelope, he took it inside the general store and handed it to the postmaster, who without so much as a "Good afternoon," took the envelope and put it to the side. Karl gave it one more look, whispered, "Good day," and left the shop, his heart much lighter. It would be a while before he could expect a reply. But a reply would come.

What Karl did not see, was his sister, Corinna, who had followed him to the post office at her mother's command. Corinna had slipped into the dark room, filled with bolts of coarse fabric, notions, and other dry goods, and a variety of scales and weights, unseen by her brother. Karl was barely out the door before her hand was on the letter, and a precious coin was left on the postmaster's counter.

"My mother's order," she said quickly, and since this was not an unknown practice, and in fact, a source of income that the postmaster looked forward to, he did not demure. Corinna, a light-footed slender girl, took a circuitous route back home, noting her unsuspecting brother in the distance. Such an innocent, she thought wryly, partly in disgust, but also envying him for not having her sly personality. She would certainly win points with her mother for bringing back this treasure, which she did not so much as glance at.

Karl took a different turn, and seemed to be walking toward the coastline, rather than returning home. It was a mild day, so welcome in this northern Baltic climate. Karl's turn toward the shore inspired Corinna to break into a run, and she was home in no time, and entered the kitchen, where her mother looked up from her accounting book.

"And?" she asked. Corinna smiled, and held the letter high. "Give that to me," the mother said. "Good girl. You left the coin?" Corinna nodded. "I won't forget this, my dear," the mother said, "now be off."

Once the door closed behind her daughter, Mrs. Amenda opened the letter and read it heartlessly. As I expected, she thought, though I was certain it was a fancy woman in that city of sin. She pressed her thin lips tightly, and squinted her eyes as she read through the note again. This will have no effect, she thought to herself. The family would continue pressing his suit of Jeanette, though it was more Jeanette's suit of Karl, and he would stay home and teach until a pastor's position became available. He was a good boy, now a good man, and this lapse would be corrected promptly. She would be sure to intercept any letters from Vienna in the future.

She held the letter in her hand a while and then crushed it in her fist. She threw it into the kitchen fire, and watched until it blackened and turned to ash. When Karl returned home, he was in a lighter mood, and spoke cheerfully to his mother, sister, and the maid. Mrs. Amenda smiled ingratiatingly and reminded him that they were to meet the Benoits in an hour. Karl smiled, a kind of far-away, knowing smile, and assented without protest. Why not, he thought. In a few weeks, I will have his reply, and I know it will be affirmative.

And Mrs. Amenda thought, "You fool. You will do exactly what I say."

Chapter 19

Despite his public proclamations of support for the General, Luis did not know what to think about Napoleon. On the one hand, he admired his brilliant audacity and energy in quashing the excesses of post-Revolutionary France. On the other, what did he really stand for? Luis's hatred of authority figures warred with his admiration for the idea of the heroic individual. Wasn't he such an individual himself? Then there was the issue of slavery. Years before, Zmeskall had teased Luis that if he returned to Bonn, the French might turn him into a slave. It was Luis's turn to laugh when Napoleon banished slavery in French colonies. However, in this new year, it would be Zmeskall's turn to say "I told you so!" when Napoleon reinstated slavery and tried to suppress the revolt of enslaved people in the Haitian Revolution. Now Austria was part of Napoleon's growing empire, but peace, at least for a few years, prevailed.

Politics was not, however, the only distraction. Luis's good friend from Bonn, Anton Reicha, a talented composer and ambitious musician just Luis's age, arrived in Vienna, and the two became close companions once again in the early months, as Luis completed his Second Symphony and other works. He was gravely disappointed when the theater director refused to allow him another benefit concert in April, which would result in a significant loss of income.

At this time another blow fell as he learned that on March 28, his dear friend Wegeler and the great love of his youth, Eleanor von Breuning, were married, as though affirming their separation from him forever. Political unrest, a significant loss of income from the concert, his growing deafness, the marriage of his two childhood friends: these elements put Luis into a spirit of gloom that no one, not even the pretty piano students, could dispel.

Various physicians attempted to provide solutions for Luis's worsening hearing, and more treatments and remedies, some laughable in their predictable futility, were prescribed. But all the doctors agreed it was time for Luis to get away again from the noise and bustle of the city, and retreat to the country for rest, quiet, and possible recuperation. In April, the essentials of the Beethoven flat were packed up and relocated a few miles to the north in the community known as "the holy city," Heiligenstadt.

Heiligenstadt was a bucolic retreat located at the foot of terraces of vineyards. Some of the finest Austrian wines came from this region, dotted with little *Heurige* (intimate wine taverns), picturesque peasant cottages with orange roofs casting stark geometric shadows across the narrow walkways, and simple white-washed churches. A hot spring and health-conscious restaurant drew hundreds of visitors, but not enough to spoil the town's secluded charm. The small town was surrounded by other villages with bell-like names: Grinzing, Nussdorf, Doebling. The clean, fresh air, the sight of workers on the hillside planting and tending the vines, an untrammeled view of the broad sky, all these things never failed to bring joy to Luis's heart, and this spring was no exception.

His refuge was a simple white-washed cottage with a wing and a courtyard that included a tree with an undulating trunk and grey pavers. Luis loved trees, and was surrounded by them in this natural place, which rekindled the love of nature he so often forgot in his daily struggles and creative efforts. But the physicians' advice was only partly true. He did benefit from the proximity to the natural world, the slower pace, the lack of interruptions. What he did not benefit from was the sense of isolation. The humming and buzzing in his ears on some days was almost unbearable, and on others, he craved even *that* sound in a prison of silence. Birds everywhere, but no songs reached his ears. The music continued in his head, and he composed much (his Triple Concerto and three additional Piano Sonatas, including the passionate "The Tempest," were among the works completed that year). But music, like steam in a kettle, must escape, and not merely by writing it out on paper.

Luis took long walks out of town, exploring the stream that led past the vine terraces, and spent more time than he should have in the *Heurige*, sampling the vineyards' bounty. But he became increasingly morose. One summer day, pounding on the piano with all his strength, alarming the landlord enough to have him rush over to observe, then be too frightened to approach the composer, Luis collapsed on the keyboard as he had as a small child in Bonn, tortured as he was then beyond endurance. This time it was not a cruel father, unless…the thought crossed his mind…God Himself was the cruel parent laughing at his tragic misfortune.

To lift his low spirits, Luis walked frequently along the brook, up toward the lowest vineyards and over a rolling hill to the next town. The sun beat hot on his face and over the summer lightened his hair, grown long with neglect. There were still groves and forests along the edges of the small agricultural communities, filled with quail, nightingales, badgers, and small deer. Luis carried his sketchbook with him, frequently stopping to record an idea or complete a musical thought. Sometimes he would get caught in a sudden rainstorm, seeking shelter beneath a stand of trees or in a church, one of the few times he would enter one as an adult, though in truth he loved the dark, cool sanctuaries of peace and stillness.

However, as the year wore on, he fell from moroseness into a deep abyss of depression. His thoughts drifted to family, always a loaded topic with Luis, which brought to mind his two younger brothers, the only close family members he had. Luis sat by the open window, day after day, obsessing with little fluctuations in his hearing, abandoning the herbal treatments and the oil. The music still pounded chaotically within his brain, like a flock of frantic, captive birds, screaming to get out.

In this black mood, unable even to compose or play, he began to write his will. But more than that, he needed to convey in the precise language of words the level of suffering that had nearly driven him to suicide.

He addressed the document to his brothers, and, after many false starts, the words flowed, as though he were taking dictation from the deepest recesses of his broken heart:

"Oh, you men who think or say that I am malevolent, stubborn, or misanthropic, how greatly do you wrong me! You do not know *the secret cause* which makes me seem that way to you. From childhood on, my heart and soul have been full of the tender feeling of goodwill, and I was ever inclined to accomplish great things.

He wrote passionately of his naturally fiery temperament, his craving for society and camaraderie. Yet, his affliction forced him further from the world's inhabitants and into unwanted solitude.

"…it was impossible for me to say to people, 'Speak louder, *shout*, for I am deaf!' Ah, how could I possibly admit an infirmity in *the one sense which ought to be more perfect in me than others*, a sense which I once possessed in the highest perfection, a perfection such as few in my profession enjoy or ever have enjoyed…"

His mind drifted back to his childhood in Bonn. In many ways, those years were the best for his intellectual development, far richer in depth, currency of knowledge, and abiding friendships than anything he had encountered in light-hearted Vienna. He recalled the long conversations with Neefe, the secret knowledge of the Illuminati, the philosophy lectures at the University, which he attended with his eager, articulate friends, the long dinnertime discussions at the von Breunings, and the books shared through the Reading Society.

These experiences informed his entire worldview and enriched his heart and mind, forming the context in which unparalleled musical expression would be shaped. Without his hearing, without the lively interaction with intelligent peers, his mind and spirit would shrivel into dust. "I live alone, almost as one who has been banished," he wrote, the quill digging deep into the vellum. He described the "hot terror" of meeting others and perhaps having them discover his condition.

"But what a humiliation for me when someone standing next to me heard a flute in the distance, and I heard nothing, or someone heard a shepherd singing and, again, I heard nothing. Such incidents drove me almost to despair; a little more of that and *I would have ended my life*. It was only my art that held me back…it seemed to me impossible to leave the world until I had brought forth all that I felt was within me…Divine One, You see my inmost soul. You know that therein dwells the love of mankind and the desire to do good…"

He then provided instructions for dividing his estate between his two brothers. "It is my wish," he wrote, "that you may have a better and freer life than I have had." Speaking to his brothers, he continued,

"Recommend *virtue* to your children; *it alone, not money, can make them happy*. I speak from experience; this was what upheld me in time of misery. Thanks to it and to my art, *I did not end my life by suicide…*"

The document was completed in early October, just as the leaves resigned themselves to the coming frost and gave off a splendor of crimson and gold before they sank dead to the earth. Scrawled on the last page, several days later, was a parting cry from the heart:

"Thus I take leave of you, and that sadly; yes, the cherished hope which I took here with me, to at least be cured to a certain degree, *it must leave me now entirely*...even the high courage which dwelt in my soul during the beautiful summer days has vanished. O Providence, let once appear to me a pure day of joy; for so long, it has been alien to me! O when, o when, o Godhead, can I feel it again in the temple of Nature and of Men? Never? No, that would be too cruel..."

His heart still heavy, Luis left his country retreat within days of writing this tortured document. While return to the city did improve his mood, a cloud of resignation and submission—themes he had underlined in the wisdom literature he valued so highly—hung over his defeated spirit. Gradually, he confided in those closest to him (his brother Carl, sometime later his brother Nicolas, and eventually some of his friends in the music business, such as Reicha, learned the erstwhile secret (patrons were to find out through gossip and innuendo). While Luis could still hear conversations and music, they were more difficult and promised a terrifying world of total silence in the years ahead.

The change of venue, however, had a positive effect on Luis's imagination. Perhaps the sharp, contrasting moods of the autumnal village and the bustling city in full artistic throttle stimulated his creative process. Luis began to enter more phrases into his sketchbook, including some ideas for a Third Symphony, something new, perhaps heroic in nature. And squabbles with publishers, some precipitated through the proactive involvement of his secretary/brother, gave him an outlet for blowing off steam. Talks developed about the composition of an opera about a courageous noble-minded heroine named Leonore (a name not so distant from Eleanor). There was even an oratorio in the works.

Spring brought Luis what was probably his greatest triumphs to date. A benefit concert was in fact mounted in April, premiering his Second Symphony, the Third Piano Concerto, *Christ on the Mount of Olives*, with the already premiered First Symphony tossed in for good measure. Luis's proceeds for this one concert equaled more than twice the annual salary of a middle-class professional at the time.

Shortly thereafter, one of the great touring virtuosos of Europe arrived in Vienna: the violinist George Bridgetower. As a young prodigy, Bridgetower had performed before Thomas Jefferson when he was visiting Paris, and throughout the European nations. Most recently he had astonished audiences in London, including many who had toasted Haydn on his two tours of England. Bridgetower was not only a technician and interpreter without rival, he also brought a personal charm, good looks, and charisma to his performances which endeared him to listeners in this most Romantic of eras. Adding to the interest in this performer was another factor: Bridgetower was black.

The violinist's mother was born in the duchy of Swabia, not far from Bavaria, but his father hailed from the West Indies and was employed in the court of Prince Esterhazy, long Haydn's patron. What thoughts crossed Bridgetower's mind as he entered Vienna in a carriage for the first time, surely being aware of the posthumous fate of another black celebrity, Angelo Soliman, in that very town.

It was his friend Ignaz Schuppenzigh, the violinist, who first alerted Luis to the arrival of Bridgetower. A gruff, solid-looking man with no interest in fashion, but a flair for networking, Schup knew both men would want to meet each other. Since they were not *both* pianists, the odds were against displays of competition and rivalry. At any rate, something good could come of this, he was sure. Schup made arrangements at the theater for the two men to meet in an informal but musical setting. Coffee, port, and pastries were set out, and Schup made sure he alone was witness to the proceedings.

Male musicians at the top of their game seldom greet each other as equals or fellow masters. More likely, there is a cagey sizing up of the other, the donning of protective armor, and making sure one's lance is sharp and ready at hand. So it was that the two men shook hands, nodded, and sat at a table with wary eyes, while Schup intercepted the server and poured them each a cup of strong coffee.

It was Bridgetower who first broke the silence.

"Beethoven," he said, leaning back and lighting a small cigarette, "I'm pleased to meet you. Your reputation extends throughout London, where I've been for several years. I've seen your first quartets, and even played one of your violin sonatas in recital. Very adventurous!"

Luis nodded, pleased by the accolades. He searched Bridgetower's face, seeing a man who was both handsome and accomplished, with graceful manners and a worldly air.

"Your reputation, too, precedes you," Luis acknowledged. "I am looking forward to hearing you tonight." The men continued with some polite, if strained, banter, but Schup was disappointed that no conversational gambit was catching fire.

"Well," said Luis, "look here! I brought some music!"

Bridgetower's eyes lit up. "Is it new?"

"You bet it's new!" said Luis, pushing the coffee to the side, splashing the tablecloth. "Here, take a look at this!" He ran a thick finger under several passages, as Bridgetower's forehead crinkled with pleasure. He reached under his chair and pulled out his violin case, removing the fine instrument (a Guarnieri), and holding it like a guitar, as the two men reviewed the passage. Bridgetower threw back his head and laughed.

"Beethoven, you fox!" he roared, "What they say about you is true. No one would change keys that many times in the opening volley!" Luis slapped Bridgetower on his back, and looked around for a piano.

"Aha, here we go, come on!" The two men scrambled like school boys over to the instrument. Schup located a music stand and quickly brought it over to the violinist, while Luis handed over his score. "I can do this from memory, not to worry," he assured his new friend.

Schup sat down across the room, ignored but glad to be so, and observed the unfolding of a new friendship and possibly a new revenue stream at his morning concert series. The two men played, and such music! A violinist of note himself, Schup was abashed at Bridgetower's effortless bowing and lyricism, the complex low notes, the high tones that seemed to fly off the soundboard like small, invisible birds. Sight-reading from manuscript, especially Luis's scrawl, was almost impossible, and yet, he and Luis were of a single mind and heart.

After their get-acquainted serenade, Bridgetower carefully placed his instrument back in its velvet-lined case, then fiercely embraced his partner-in-music.

"You are unsurpassed, George!" exclaimed Luis. "I've never heard such playing!" Though in fact, he heard only the lower tones.

"And you! Magnificent!" exclaimed Bridgetower, laughing. "You must write something for me. Should it be a commission?"

"No, no, no, just a tribute from one artist to another," insisted Luis, who found he could understand more when he observed the lips of the speaker. This was the best he had felt since long before he went to the country the previous spring. See, he said to his inner demons, see what a little appreciation can do!

"I have some notes for a new violin sonata, undoubtedly my finest," said Luis, "and the dedication page will bear your name!" The two men chatted, then broke into a session of improvisations and some silly songs, until Luis announced he had better attend to his compositions or they would have nothing worthwhile to play in the future.

The next few weeks offered no rest from the completed benefit concert. In addition to lessons for the boy Czerny and the usual assortment of fetching ladies, Luis had taken the son of his old mentor Franz Ries under his wing. The young Ries, a handsome young man named Ferdinand, was taking lessons in composition as well as piano, and provided yet another comforting link to his early friends in Bonn. But there was so much music to compose. Schup had given him a deadline for late May to complete the sonata for a breakfast concert series at the ungodly hour of 8 a.m. Luis was notorious for working right up to the very last minute, and this episode was to be no different. The ink was still wet on the violinist's score when Luis arrived just under the wire in a disheveled but upbeat state on the morning of the 24th.

Bridgetower was a little annoyed to be kept waiting, and not to have a clue as to the sonata in advance. Still, sight-reading was one of the ways he could dazzle audiences with his genius, so he elegantly smoothed the pages on his stand, glanced through the score with widening eyes, and finally bent over to murmur one word in Luis's ear: "Long!" And again, "Love the double stops!"

This was in fact the longest violin sonata in history (at that time), and the most complex and engaging, the famous sonata in A major (though even the key is open to dispute, since Luis did not clearly indicate a key signature). As audience members rubbed their wakening eyes, the two musicians launched into a spirited performance of the Violin Sonata No. 9, rendered more energetic by the close call of nearly not playing at all.

The audience cheered vigorously, for it was remarkable music, and both musicians were consummate showmen, though Luis kept his hands close to the keyboard as was his style. After rounds of congratulations, and a few stops to chat with a music journalist and a publisher's agent, the two went back to Luis's flat to review a few rough places in the score, then out for a late mid-day meal at The Swan.

"Ah," sighed the violinist, throwing back his head in relief, "that was fantastic. But I'm glad it's behind us. I'd like to take this on the road, Beethoven. What are you doing in the next few months?"

Luis laughed gruffly. "I'm afraid I can't leave just yet. Commissions, patrons, problems with publishers, that sort of thing."

"Too bad," said Bridgetower, lighting a thin cigarette, "We get along, our performing styles are in sync. Look, we even match!" he noted with a wink, holding his hand next to Luis's.

"So true, on all scores!" the composer added. He seemed a bit distracted, even glum after the morning's brilliant start, Bridgetower thought. Perhaps he needs a little diversion to put him in a sweeter mood.

The restaurant was filling up with customers on the pleasant spring afternoon, and Bridgetower cast his eye on a number of good-looking women, several in a party by themselves, another with a man who left to conduct business with a colleague.

"Look over there, Luis," he said. "Now that is one handsome wench." Luis looked in the indicated direction, and was surprised to see none other than Anna Milder, already a celebrated soprano at age 17 and a student of Luis's own teachers, Salieri and Haydn.

"I wouldn't bother with her," said Luis uneasily, trying to distract his dining companion. "She's too young, and from what I hear, can be very loud!" But Luis's reaction had exactly the opposite effect on George Bridgetower.

"What is it, Luis, is she too much the woman for you? Eh?" Bridgetower turned to continue admiring the young woman, and trying to catch her eye. "Too young? This from the man who was seduced by a 16-year-old Galician?" he added, referring to Luis's flirtation with Julie Guicciardi.

"She's too well known around town," said Luis guardedly. "She is a true artist! You are asking for trouble," he added. Bridgetower liked seeing Luis squirm; this was a side of the master he had not yet seen, and it was most entertaining.

"I think she likes me," he said, beaming. "In fact, I think I'm going to go over there and introduce myself!"

"You'll do nothing of the sort!" shouted Luis, slamming his fist on the table. "I said," he lowered his voice and pulled his collar a bit higher, "Leave. Her. Alone!"

With this Bridgetower arose, brushed off his lapels and sleeves, looked at Luis, then at the attractive patron, who noticed a tiff at the distant table and was frowning as she tried to recognize the parties, a feat exacerbated by nearsightedness.

"Beethoven, I think you are jealous, I do, I do," purred the incomparable violinist. "I am going over there right now before her companion returns, and I will bring her back here and introduce her to you!"

With this, Luis flew into a rage, grabbed Bridgetower by both shoulders and pushed him down into the seat, while trying to keep his back to the lovely Anna.

"Let's go!" he said in no uncertain terms. As his colleague demurred, Luis slammed a plate on the table, reached over and grabbed the score of the violin sonata from Bridgetower's pocket, and, shaking it, shouted, "Not for you! You are no friend of mine!" and awkwardly dashed from the restaurant, tails flying, fingers crushing the edges of the score. Anna never did know who was making a scene on the other side of the room, and good thing, since she was destined to star in Luis's opera, *Fidelio*, a few years later. For his part, Bridgetower simply took a deep breath, accepted the sympathetic glances and expressions of those nearby, settled into his chair, and ordered a brandy.

Luis, on the other hand, was livid, and later, while he had forgotten the reason for the disturbance, did not forget that Bridgetower was the object of his ire. Back in his room, he told Ries to contact another violinist, Rudolf Kreutzer, and let him know that he, not George, would receive the dedication. "Bridgetower is dead!" Luis exclaimed, pushing a stack of sketchbooks and scores to the floor. And though, as it would turn out, the new honoree would not like and would refuse to play the composition, it would be known throughout the ages as the Kreutzer, rather than the Bridgetower, Sonata.

Chapter 20

The squabble in the restaurant was not the reason Luis was on edge. Before he entered The Swan that day, something was already grinding within him, like a succubus gnawing on the marrow of his bones. He couldn't put his finger on it, but it was there, a relentless, burning, seething, smoldering something not quite ready to catch fire.

He had felt that sensation before in his life, and in truth, it was when he felt most vitally alive, but never quite like this. He dismissed Ries, told Czerny's father to take the lad home, there would be no lesson that week, or perhaps the next. Carl, who hadn't been feeling well, knew it was best to leave alone the older brother with the unspecified focus in his eyes. The buzzing sensation moved from his brain into his heart, to his groin, down his arms until his broad flat fingertips vibrated and burned, down his legs into his feet, which grew hot. It was as though the ringing in his ears had taken a sensory turn and flooded his entire nervous system with vibrating fire.

Eventually, he dowsed his head and hands with a pitcher of water. Drying himself on his scarf, he took several of the sketchbooks from the floor, and thumbed through them, in search of something, he did not know what. Looking, looking. The answer was there, he felt it. Some note, some phrase, a rhythmic pattern, a progression.

He closed the books, and sat staring out the window, into the afternoon, the evening, the night. The cook had left his dinner, which grew cold. He poured a glass of claret and eventually, rolled over on the sofa and fell asleep. He dreamed, long, disturbing, sometimes violent dreams, dreams of places he had been as a child, and doors that were closed to him, the great doors of a large church that he could not budge, the elegant door of a court salon with haughty servants blocking his passage, the rough doors to a stable that he could not open, though he heard the neighs of horses near on the other side.

In his dream, he ran down a narrow street that wound and twisted but seemed to lead nowhere, looking back over his shoulder at the unidentified form of someone in hot pursuit. He ran and ran, and found himself suddenly in a forest at the top of a hill, and dawn was breaking, and the brilliant light of a miracle sky—like a Baroque depiction of heaven with rays of sunshine and fluttering birds—flooded his path. His hand now was on a bridle and he was pulling with all his strength at a great black stallion who reared and kicked and snorted, but he would not let go, he could not let go.

As he reached up and grasped the beast's black mane with his last breath, he jolted awake and let out a loud cry. Luis was panting, and sweat ran down his back. Shaking from the images, so real, so completely consuming, he lit a lantern, and took a sketchbook over to the piano. Finishing the remaining wine in one gulp, he sat on the piano bench, his fingers fell on a series of chords in E flat, then a jarring C# and he began to hammer away at the scraps of sound that would evolve into a new symphony, his most remarkable and controversial to date.

When it was complete and he played it on the piano for Ries, easily the most intelligent and appreciative of his friends and students, the young man had to steady himself as he sank slowly to the chair beside the master. In 50 minutes, easily twice the length of a classical symphony, the work not only broke new ground for musical expression: in a sense, all great music from that moment onward would trace its origin to this single liberating work.

"It is by his own statement the greatest work he has yet written," Ries soon wrote to the publisher and Bonn friend, Simrock. "Beethoven recently played it to me, and I think that heaven and earth must tremble beneath one's feet in a performance. He has a great desire to dedicate it to Bonaparte."

The symphony consisted of four interrelated sections originating from a sweeping, heroic first movement. The second movement offered a solemn funeral march, perhaps symbolic of the hero's transition to a state of immortality, ending in musical sobs of despair as the orchestra itself seems to unravel and collapse in on itself. The third movement suggested renewal, perhaps even resurrection, followed by a roar of triumph in the fourth movement finale built upon themes used earlier in the *Creatures of Prometheus* ballet. Bonaparte indeed! And it was audacious for Luis to suggest this dedication, since many of his patrons were staunchly anti-French, and Austria would once again soon be at war with Napoleon's forces. But was the symphony really "about" Bonaparte after all?

Conceived during the tortured final days at Heiligenstadt the previous year, the work seemed to mirror the turmoil Luis had experienced on every level following the loss of hearing and of love. Was the funeral march and the complete dissolution of the orchestra in those final measures, in fact the expiration of the composer himself? And was he able, through music, to resurrect himself as a new creature, perhaps a creature of Prometheus, who defied the gods to bring light and understanding to humankind? (His ballet, *The Creatures of Prometheus*, had premiered just three years before.)

As though by miracle, a maelstrom of creative energy swept through the composer. In the following winter came sketches for works which would come to be known as masterpieces of world music for all time: the Fifth and Sixth Symphonies, the Waldstein and Appassionata Piano Sonatas, the Fourth Piano Concerto, and many other works. Tributes and commissions began to pour in, including the gift of a new Erard piano from Paris, complete with four pedals and additional keys (though Luis did not like the instrument's sluggish "action" and preferred the pianos made by his old friend Streicher). And while the love of a potential marriage partner still eluded him, Luis enjoyed the solicitous attention of his sometime host, the Princess Marie Erdödy of Budapest.

Creativity kept the demons at bay, perhaps transforming them into art, which others in turn could access for inspiration as they engaged in psychological and spiritual warfare of their own.

In the spring, however, the Theater on the Wien, where Luis had been in residence, came under new management, and the composer had to move out. He found new lodgings in the southern part of the city. He was between projects, preparing for the publication of the Third Symphony, when Ries burst into the room in a state of agitation.

"Sir, you are not going to believe this!" exclaimed Ries, dashing to the piano where Luis sat. "It's Bonaparte. He has declared himself Emperor!"

As a black storm cloud sweeps across a clear May sky, blotting out the sun, Luis's face changed from a cheerful expression of friendly greeting to a dark and threatening squall of violent emotions.

"What are you saying?"

"I said, Bonaparte has declared himself Emperor! He has betrayed all who trusted in him. He who would end tyranny *has himself become a tyrant*!"

In his need to urgently communicate important news, Ries had not thought through the consequences of his announcement. No sooner had the words left his lips, than Ries was overcome with regret at his rashness. The composer looked like he was about to explode. And then he did.

"This can't be true!" Luis roared, bounding from the bench, and dashing the score he was working on onto the floor. He walked back and forth briskly, holding his head in his hands, kicking inanimate objects out of his way, then stood facing the window, both fists pounding on the wall. "No, no, no!"

"Master, I'm sorry I was so abrupt. Here, sit down," offered Ries, trying to calm his teacher and friend. Luis was now hitting his head against the windowpane, and Ries was attempting to pull him back. The servant ran in from the kitchen, but Ries shooed him away. "Sir, please calm down, the people will not stand for this. Austria, the German states, will not stand for this, it will not last for long, I am certain!"

"Where did you hear this?" fumed Luis, not moving.

"There is nothing else in the papers, nor on people's lips," said Ries, his voice rising so the master would hear each word. "It is a fact. But it will not be endured."

Luis turned, his face flushed with rage, every muscle and tendon in his body tight with anger. "To think I was duped," he said, his back to the wall. "To think I believed and trusted…that!" The composer's eyes then fixed on a table across the room from the two men.

"Well," he said, regaining some composure and trying to breathe deeply. "There is *some*thing I can do!" He strode across the room, walking right over scores, newspapers, and kicking a tray of dishes to the side.

He stood at the table where lay a single thick document. It was the autograph original of the Third Symphony. Ries, who was close behind him, looked down as Luis put both hands firmly on the table edge for support. "Sir, what are you thinking?" Ries asked fearfully, hoping to stop some dire action.

Luis reached down and lifted up the first section attached to the title page. Luis's name was written on the bottom of the sheet. At the top, in large ornate script, was a single word. That word was *Bonaparte*.

Luis snatched the pages faster than Ries could react and tore them down the center and threw the pieces onto the floor. Ries gasped. Luis breathed out, hard and with a sense of finality. The student did not dare to pick up the pieces or even to move.

"It is over," said Luis, returning to a kind of post-apocalyptic calm. "So he is no more than a common mortal!" Luis said, walking back to the window and speaking to himself rather than to Ries. "Now he, too, will tread under foot all the rights of man, indulge only his ambition. Now he will think himself superior to all men. A tyrant!"

Ries had the cowering servant bring Luis a glass of Rhine wine, and mustered the nerve to lead his teacher to a comfortable chair.

"All my life," Luis said, again to himself, "all my life, it has been a struggle. Why am I always the odd man out? What does it mean, Ries? Like all men, I seek a hero to show me the way. Here was one. And now we see he has feet of clay. Whom can we turn to?" He stopped and had a drink of wine, motioning to the servant to bring a glass for Ries.

"I think I know," he said at last. "The answer isn't there," he pointed out the window, "but here," he pointed to his heart and head, much as he had to Neefe so many years ago. "Knowledge and wisdom, reason and faith. But always, our own self-determination." He was silent for a while, and Ries made no motion. "Ries, you may go, no lessons today. Well, no *music* lessons, at any rate!" patting the young man on the back, sending him out.

Luis sat alone on this beautiful May morning, his hearing more than half gone, but his other senses sharp and alert. The world made a peculiar sense, for the first time. He realized with utter clarity that one could not put their trust entirely in man, any man. His thoughts drifted from the world of politics to his own life.

Why was I Black in a White world? Why did I have typhus and small pox, and why did I survive and others not? Why was I short and smaller than others? Why was everything destroyed in the fire and the flood? Why did I have a cruel father who beat me? Why did my mother die? Why was I gifted when others were not?

What does it mean to be alien in one's own land, by an accident of birth and then, no accident, but deliberate ostracism and sometimes persecution and sometimes abandonment into the incomparable aloneness of the Self?

When I stood in the woods beyond the vineyards, when I stood and thought how simple it would be to lie down—never to rise, to let starvation and thirst remove me from the torments of a life of difference—when I had in that manner considered ending my life, it was not because of deafness, it was because I had given up the struggle to overcome the sense of otherness that followed me since birth.

The whispers about an earlier child born with the same name, the racial ambiguity, the lies about my age. An infant has no defense against a judging world and all its creatures pass judgment and want to block out this oddity from the predictable flow of things, the natural order. A mother, or midwife, intervenes, but the other does not disappear. Indeed, the only recourse is to embrace the alien Self.

I have been shipwrecked in a foreign land, and it was the land of my birth and the land to which I fled. Estranged from man, from God, from all Creation, I am cast out in unfamiliar waters to fend for myself, and, despite the best efforts of all, I have not failed. I have not failed!

Like the master of a martial art, I have turned the force of my opponents back upon themselves until it is the *status quo* that trembles. Has this occurred before? I would be self-centered to think so. But for me—no, it has not occurred before—and so this is something entirely new—the strangeness of my music, of this particular symphony, of my own identity.

For now I see who I am, I see it written on these sounds I can barely hear but which will ring out for all eternity. I am engraved on every invisible note and encoded in every silent chord. And still it is a kind of heroism, but not in the realm of politics or art: it embodies the moment when the odd man out confronts his destiny and says to the legion of those who would obstruct him, "I have taken Fate by the throat! It will not bend and crush me."

And with this, and with a new name, the name of the disenfranchised rather than a self-proclaimed ruler of men, the name "Eroica," *heroic,* I rededicate this symphony and light the flame, not for one fallible man, but for the hope of all, for all Eternity.

Acknowledgments

Acknowledgment does not suggest that the individuals who have assisted or inspired me necessarily support this project or endorse this novel, which blends fact with fiction. However, they were kind and generous in sharing resources and providing insight (and in some cases, inspiration) regarding the life, community, and music of Beethoven. I am deeply grateful to:

The University of Bonn Archives, Thomas Becker, director

The Ira F. Brilliant Center for Beethoven Studies at San José State,

William Meredith, director and scholar-in-residence, and

Patricia Stroh, curator

The Beethoven-Haus Bibliothek, Bonn, Germany, Dorothea Geffert, librarian

Sarada Holt Johnson for her encouragement, patience, and understanding

Readers Marguerite Auerbacher and Julia Pillard for their keen powers of observation, invaluable critical review, and warm support.

The Burlington County, New Jersey, Public Library System

Alan Morrison, the Haas Charitable Trust Chair in Organ Studies, the Curtis Institute of Music

Terry Melanson, author, *The Perfectibilists*, Trine Day (January 31, 2009)

Londa Schwiebinger, the John L. Hinds Professor of History of Science, Stanford University, author of "The Anatomy of Difference: Race and Gender in Eighteenth-Century Science," *Eighteenth-Century Studies,* Summer 1990

Jonathan Biss, pianist, author, and educator, The Curtis Institute of Music, whom I met through a Coursera course on Beethoven's Piano Sonatas

An expression of deepest gratitude to the late Susanne Zantop, author of the incomparable essay, "The Beautiful, the Ugly, and the German Race: Gender and Nationality in Eighteenth-Century Anthropological Discourse." Dr. Zantop's essay can be found in the anthology, *Gender and Germanness, Cultural Productions of Nation.* Berghahn Books, 1987.

Biographical material absorbed over a lifetime of reading includes a number of works, led by the gold standard of Beethoven research, *The Life of Beethoven* by Alexander Wheelock Thayer. Other authors whose works I consulted in the final stages of writing included Barry Cooper, Maynard Solomon, and popular Beethoven Web sites such as the Raptus Society, Ludwig van Beethoven Forum, and the Beethoven Reference Site. A number of Web sites provided public-domain translations of Beethoven documents, sufficient for a work of fiction, though not for scholarship. I have not read any work of fiction about Beethoven, though I have enjoyed a couple of films, especially *Copying Beethoven*, with a commendable performance by Ed Harris.

For those wondering which episodes in this novel were purely fictional, they include the Masonic reunion and any connection between Beethoven and his cousin Rovantini with the racial experiment at Kassel. However, both episodes have a deep connection to Beethoven's story. Masonic life was an important part of the world of Beethoven and his mentors. His teacher Neefe, briefly mentioned in this book, was head of the Bonn chapter of the Bavarian Illuminati, another secret society popular in the late eighteenth century. As for the experiment at Kassel, it underscores just how entrenched racism and discrimination against dark-skinned people was during the years of Beethoven's development. Another fictional episode relates to the Immortal Beloved. We may never know for certain who the beloved was, but we do know that Beethoven's heart was captured by a friend he knew for too short a time.